CW00539393

A dark corner

The bell rings on a wet evening in a north-west London suburb. Nelly Didcot, though her legs are bad, makes it through the crowded furniture of the kitchen and along the passage to the front door. It is a tall young man, wet through and coughing, asking about a room. He has come to the wrong address . . . 'but you wouldn't turn a dog out on a night like this'. Mrs Didcot offers him an armchair in the kitchen. Just for the night.

So begins Errol's relationship with Nelly and Arthur Didcot, which builds, by way of the most ordinary and friendly events, to a horrifying and murderous climax.

Celia Dale excels at the chilling detail, the depiction of the horror that can lurk beneath the cosiest of façades. In this beautifully economical crime novel, first published in 1971, she surpasses herself, placing her three characters with perfect precision in their social setting, and weaving together two closely twined and compelling stories—the revelation of a dreadful truth between the veneer of respectability, and the gradual growth of understanding and of love.

Also by Celia Dale

The least of these
To hold the mirror
The dry land
The wooden O
Trial of strength
A spring of love
Other people
A helping hand
Act of love
The innocent party
Helping with enquiries

Celia Dale

A dark corner

Constable London

First published in Great Britain 1971
by Macmillan London Ltd

Reprinted 1985
by Constable & Company Ltd
10 Orange Street, London WC2H 7EG
Printed in Great Britain by
St Edmundsbury Press
Bury St Edmunds, Suffolk

ISBN 0 09 466300 9

To Juliet O'Hea,
good friend

ONE

It took Mrs Didcot some time to get to the front door, partly because, as usual, she had the radio on and did not at first hear the bell, partly because, when she did, she thought it was children playing tricks again, and partly because her legs were bad and it was difficult for her to move at all, especially between the crowded furniture of the kitchen. As she supported herself round the table the knocker fell twice, gently. 'All right, all right,' she muttered, 'I'm coming.' She got into the passage and eased herself along it, hearing the letterbox flap rattle and then the bell again. 'Who can that be? All right, I'm coming . . .' She reached the door and opened it.

It was an overcast evening and pouring with rain, so that she shuffled back a step, half-closing the door against the deluge and the tall, dark figure which said, with white teeth, 'I've come about the room.'

'What's that? What room? We haven't got no room.'

'It says on this paper there's a room.'

'What paper?' She opened the door a bit and leaned forward, peering at the paper held out to her by a dark hand. The rain spattered her face and the young man coughed, hunching his shoulders.

'I haven't got my glasses. What's it say, then?'

'It says you've got a room.'

'It can't do. Here, you'd better come in.' She moved back, steadying herself on the door handle, and the man stepped in. He began to cough again, bringing out a handkerchief and holding it to his mouth. She reached out and switched on the light, weakly harsh in its warped shade. The young man had nothing on his head and the rain sparkled on the close black hair and the shoulders of his plastic lumberjacket; his jeans were soaked dark.

'What's it say, then?' she repeated.

'It says "Room to let, no facilities, reasonable, apply Johnson 6 Wardlow Crescent".'

'This isn't Wardlow Crescent. This is Wardlow Road. You got the wrong address.'

'You don't have no room?'

'No, dear, you got the wrong address. Where'd you get that paper, then?'

'The newspaper shop at the corner. I bin to two others but they said they was let. Where's Wardlow Crescent, then?'

'It's the other way, up past the Conveniences and round on the left and then it's just past the Odeon. You could take the bus.'

'No, I'll find it.' He wiped his face and his head and put the handkerchief away.

She looked him over. 'That's a shocking cough you got there.'

'It's okay.'

'You don't look too good. Would you like a cup of tea?'

He nodded.

'Come on, then.' She turned and began to shuffle along the hall. 'I'm a bit slow because of my legs.'

They came slowly into the kitchen, where the radio still chatted and a stronger light shone down on a litter of saucepans, crockery, newspapers, ornaments. The room was warm, for the gas fire gave out a hoarse heat.

'You sit by the fire, dear, and get yourself warm. What a night, eh? You wouldn't believe it was August. Nice weather for ducks, my Gran always said, and I used say Well, it's all right for the ducks.' She moved about, filling the kettle, setting it on a roaring gas, rinsing a dirty cup and finding a second one, spooning tea into a big brown teapot with a rubber spout.

The youth sat hunched to the fire, holding out his long fingers to its heat, his knees sharp in the jeans which had begun to steam a little. His face had a mauvish tint and from time to time he shivered.

Propped up against the table waiting for the kettle to boil, she stared at him. 'You're looking for a room, then?'

'That's right.'

'Well, you come to the wrong address. Wardlow Crescent's what it says there.'

'Yes. You know it?'

'I know Wardlow Crescent but I don't know no Johnsons. They're all new people round here now, I don't know none of them, and of course I don't get out much, not with my legs. We used to know a nice lot of people, real neighbours they were, when my mother was alive. Lived here all her life, she had, hardly ever bin up to the West End till she was married. Not in this house, of course, in one of them little cottages got bombed in the war, round King's Crescent. We'd moved here before that, though. When us kids started coming they needed more room, see, and you could buy one of these houses for a couple of hundred pounds. Won't bear thinking of, will it? They earned good money too, master joiners did – that's what my dad was, a master joiner, a real craftsman. Not what you'd call real money now, but it did us all right and we've still got the house. Where d'you come from?'

'Wolverhampton.'

'No, I mean where was you born?'

'I told you – Wolverhampton.'

He began to cough again, sinking his head between his shoulders so that he seemed curled in over his chest. The kettle screamed and she filled the teapot, reaching across the draining-board for the milk bottle, and then easing her way round the table to her armchair by the fire.

'You ought to do something about that cough.'

'First I got to find a room.'

'Haven't you got no home, then?'

He shook his head and, reaching into his tight jeans, got out the handkerchief again and wiped his mouth.

'You ought to undo that jacket, you won't get the benefit else. How d'you like it?'

'As it comes.'

As she poured out the tea and pushed it across to him, he straightened up and unzipped the lumber-jacket. A striped T-shirt covered his thin chest. He took the cup and poured milk into it, the bottle clinking against the rim. She could see he was clenching his teeth to prevent them chattering. He wrapped his hands round the cup and took a sip.

'You on your own, then?'

'That's right.'

'Where you bin living?'

'Here and there. I had a room but I didn't like the people.'

'But you got a bed somewhere?' He shook his head. 'No bed? You mean you bin running around with that cough and nowhere to sleep?'

'I'm looking for a room.'

'Well, you are a silly juggins, aren't you? Fancy not having nowhere to sleep with a cough like that!'

'Last night I kipped down in the grocery van but the guvnor don't know and if he found out, I'd get my cards.'

'You're working then?'

'Warehouseman at Mansfield Groceries in the High Street. Started yesterday. So I need a room somewhere round here.'

'Well, you got the wrong address.'

There was silence, save for the dialogue of the radio against which their own had been pitched and the occasional beat of rain on the window. From the sags and bulges of her chair, moulded over the years to fit her own contours, Mrs Didcot scrutinised her visitor. The tea did not seem to have done him much good but had merely heightened the glitter in his eyes and brought sweat out on the face that, as she stared at it, seemed to grow greyer and greyer. Rigidly though he held himself, he was shivering, and the cough took him again. She heaved herself forward and removed his cup, refilling it and adding several spoonfuls of sugar before setting it on the table near him. When the paroxysm was over he wiped his face and hands and leaned back in the hard chair, closing his eyes.

'I tell you what,' she said, 'you sit there quietly till my hubby gets home. We haven't really got no room, not to let that is, but you can't go running around with that cough in this weather. Or any other, come to that.'

'I'll be okay.'

'Not with that cough, you won't. It's my belief you've got a temperature. Haven't you got no family?'

'Not here.'

'Well, you take off that jacket and those wet shoes and just sit there quietly till my hubby gets back. Here, you wrap this round you.'

From beneath the cushions at her back she extracted a shawl of knitted squares, brightly variegated and clumsily sewn together. He slowly took off his lumber-jacket, folding it back over the wooden chair. As he bent down to unlace the canvas track-shoes, she stretched forward and placed the shawl over his peaked shoulders. There was a hole in one of his socks.

Arthur Didcot returned at eleven o'clock, as was his custom. He let himself in quietly and hung his cap and raincoat on the hall stand. As he did so, his wife called from the front room. 'Is that you, Dad?'

'Hullo?' Her door was ajar and he pushed it open. 'I didn't expect you to still be awake. Anything up?'

She heaved herself up a bit in the double bed, which almost filled the room. 'I stayed awake special. There's a young chap in the kitchen.'

'A young chap?'

'Yes. He come about a room.'

'We haven't got no room.'

'No, I told him. He had the wrong address. He's got ever such a shocking cough, poor boy, so I said he could stay. Just for the night.'

He regarded her silently for a moment out of his rather prominent eyes. 'That was a silly thing to do.'

'It was coming down cats and dogs.'

'Where is he?'

'He's dossed down in my chair under the blanket. He was ever so poorly, you couldn't turn a dog out in a night like this. Is it still raining?'

'No. You took a chance, Mother.'

'He's ever such a nice young chap. You can tell. All on his own and nowhere to sleep and that shocking cough. You'd have done the same.'

'I don't know about that. Well, I'd best have a look at him.'

She lifted a hand. 'There's just one thing.'

'What's that?'

'He's a darkie.'

'A darkie?'

'Yes, dear. But he's ever so clean.'

'I don't want no darkies in my house.'

'You wouldn't notice it, Dad, he speaks just the same as we do. He was born in Wolverhampton.'

'One of old Enoch's lot, eh?'

'I suppose so. Anyway, he's all on his own down here with nowhere to sleep and that shocking cough.'

'And no cash neither, I daresay.'

'I didn't ask, dear, but he's got a job. At Mansfield's in the High Street.'

'Has he?' He stood for a moment then allowed a smile to soften his bony face. 'You're a prize packet and no mistake. You'll have us all murdered in our beds one day.'

She smiled back. 'I knew you'd take it all right, Dad. He's only young.'

'So are them skinheads and hippies and student power. All young people are tearaways these days, that's what's wrong with this country. Well, never mind, I daresay we'll survive for one night. I'll have a look at him, though.'

'Don't wake him up, dear. He needs to sleep it out.'

'And so do you. You ought to've bin asleep long ago. Have you had your pills?'

'I'll have them now. I didn't want to go off before you came home so's I could tell you.'

'Well, you certainly told me.' Indulgently he watched her rummage in the litter on the bamboo table by her bed and swallow two pills. The bed, a huge mahogany wardrobe and dressing-table, almost filled the room, and every corner and surface was crammed with clothes, old magazines, framed photographs, medicine bottles, all easily to hand without having to open drawers and cupboards.

She lay back on the pillows. 'Goodnight then, dear. Sleep tight.'

'Make sure the bugs don't bite.' He switched off the light and she smiled at the ritual words, closing her eyes on the darkness.

He shut the door carefully and stood for a moment in the passage, pursing his lips as he always did when thoughtful; then, cautiously opening the kitchen door, he peered inside. By the weakly reflected light from the hall he could see the youth fast asleep in Nelly's chair. He was huddled sideways, his knees drawn up, covered to his shoulders by the knitted blanket. His head drooped down against the upholstery, precariously hung on a slender neck, and he was snoring. In the almost darkness his face was too dark to see, but his shape was meek and vulnerable.

Arthur Didcot clicked his tongue, shook his head a little, shut the door quietly and then, on a moment's thought, locked it and put the key on the hall stand. Then he went out to the dank lavatory just outside the back door, pissed delicately, pulled the rusty plug, sniffed the night air scented with rain and, faintly, urine, came inside, locked the back door, and went upstairs to his own neat quarters.

The youth awoke in almost the same position in which he had fallen asleep. He groaned and unbent his limbs painfully, raising his head to find himself regarded from the other side of the table by a small, thin man with grey hair parted in the middle. He jerked upright and Mr Didcot smiled, showing plastic teeth.

'Morning, son. Had a good sleep?'

He mumbled something, pushing the blanket aside and straightening his legs.

'I'm Mr Didcot. Mother told me we'd got an orphan of the storm.'

He looked round for her but Mr Didcot shook his head. 'She don't get up first thing. I let her have her sleep out, poor old girl. She needs it, with her legs. Would you like a cup of tea?'

'Yes.'

'Kettle's just on the boil. How're you feeling this morning?'

'Okay, I think. I slept a treat.'

'You looked cosy enough.'

'The lady give me a pill, I flaked right out.' He stood up, hitching his jeans, and the movement made him cough.

Mr Didcot spooned tea into the pot. 'The toilet's out the back.'

'Okay.' He went out, and while he was gone Mr Didcot quickly examined the lumberjacket which still hung over the wooden chairback. There was nothing in the pockets save a dirty handkerchief, a few coins, and a piece of paper with the advertisement for a room written on it. He was folding the blanket when the young man returned.

'You can have a wash in the sink.'

'Okay.' He edged round the table and turned on the tap, sluicing his face with cold water with gaspings and bubblings and a recurrence of the cough. Mr Didcot handed him a towel, then made the tea.

'That's a nasty cough you got.'

'I'm okay. I don't have no fever now. What time is it?'

Mr Didcot took a watch out of the pocket of the waistcoat that hung open over his shirt and, holding it at arm's length, studied it. 'Seven and a half minutes to eight o'clock.'

'I got to be at work at half past.'

'You fit to go?'

The young man smiled, taking the cup Mr Didcot pushed over to him and wrapping both hands round it. 'I better be. I only started Monday.'

'That's the spirit.' Mr Didcot sat down and stirred his tea. 'You don't get enough of it these days. There's too much of this world-owes-me-a-living attitude these days, young chaps going on National Assistance rather than do an honest day's work. Absenteeism, strikes, restrictive practices – there's no one prepared to do an honest day's work for a day's pay these days. Working at Mansfield's, are you?'

'That's right.'

'Decent firm, I should say.'

'They seem okay.'

'Where were you before, then?'

'Here and there. I don't have no proper trade. I was on the Underground for a while.'

'They use a lot of you chaps, London Transport does. They do say the trains couldn't run if it wasn't for all of you. Them racialists don't take that into account.'

'The smell turned me up. And the people just shoving their tickets at you like you was dirt . . .' He took a gulp of tea.

'There's no consideration for others these days. Before the war people had consideration. There wasn't all this pushing and grabbing and I'm-all-right-Jack. It's every man for himself these days and devil take the hindmost. Mother said you're on your own.'

'That's right.'

'No family?'

'Not here.'

'Wolverhampton, wasn't it?'

He nodded.

'Struck off on your own, then?'

'That's right.'

They finished their tea in silence, the youth's eyes downcast, withdrawn into his thin dark body as into a cave. Mr Didcot studied him – the close round head, the smooth brown planes of the face, young but not now glossed with health, the neat nose, broad lips, the deep eye sockets whose lids closed up the whole face; the slender neck and angular shoulders, long torso on long legs that seemed, even in repose, ready to move. There were plenty enough of them in the streets, heaven knows, but never before had there been so good an opportunity to stare.

The youth finished his tea and put the cup on the

table. 'I'd better be moving.' He stood up and again the cough awoke.

'You want to watch out for that cough.'

'It's warm in the store.'

'Well, you want to take care.'

He began to put on the lumberjacket. 'Will you tell the lady thanks for letting me stay?'

'I will. You go after that room in your dinner break, I would. You got the wrong address last night.'

'Yes. She told me where to go.'

He zipped up the jacket and moved round towards the door. Mr Didcot got up and followed him into the hall.

'Keep your chest covered up.'

A grey sky was reflected in puddles and wet pavements. Beyond the overgrown hedge a bus hissed by, full up and impervious to the Request stop a few yards along the road. From the nearby building site a hooter blew for the start of the day's work.

The young man raised a hand in farewell and pulled the front door shut behind him. Mr Didcot went back into the kitchen, switched on the radio and fried himself an egg.

Just before six that evening the bell rang. Mr Didcot went to answer it, then came back into the kitchen saying, 'Look who's here.' His wife struggled forward from the billows of her chair as the young man followed him in. His face was grey, his shoulders hunched as he coughed and coughed, and he sank down on the nearest chair and rested his head in his hands.

'My word,' she said, 'you do look queer!'

He nodded, recovering himself slowly, sitting up and wiping his face with his crumpled handkerchief. 'I just lasted out the day. I didn't know what to do.'

'Give him a cup of tea, Dad.'

The remains of their meal were still on the table. Mr Didcot looked inside the teapot, then got a cup and filled it with warm liquid, pushing it across the table. The youth took it, shivering.

'You've got a temperature again,' she said.

He smiled wanly, and took a sip.

Mr Didcot sat down and studied him. 'Did you go after that room?'

He nodded. 'In my dinner break. It was no good.'

'Gone?'

He shrugged. 'So they said. They didn't even let me over the step.'

'What you going to do, then?'

'I don't know.' His head drooped over the cup and he closed his eyes.

Mrs Didcot looked at her husband, who continued to study the youth. 'He'll have to stay, Dad.'

'I don't know where.'

'Just for a night or two, till that cough's eased up a bit.'

'But where we going to put him?'

'In the Den?'

'Certainly not! I'm not going to have no one messing about in the Den, you know better than that.'

'There's the attic.'

There was a pause while Mr Didcot thought, pursing his lips and playing a little tune on the table with his fingers, still studying the youth, who seemed to have fallen asleep. His breathing was noisy.

Mrs Didcot edged forward coaxingly. 'There's that old camp bed we never got rid of from the ARP. He could doss down on that and he'd be in nobody's way. We can't turn him out like this, Dad, it'd be inhuman.'

'We don't know nothing about him.'

'You can see he's a nice young chap – he can't help his colour. And he's weak as a kitten with that cough.'

'He might murder us in our beds.'

'What, him?' She leaned back and the mounds and folds of her face and body shook gently with laughter. 'Go on, Dad, you know you'd never forgive yourself if you turned him out, not the condition he's in. And he worked out the day, too, not like some would.'

'That's true enough.' He pondered, staring at the drooping figure, graceful even in its ungainliness, its strange small head, colour, shape. 'Very well, Mother, you have your way. But it's only till he can find somewhere else, mind.'

'That's my Arthur.'

The hall floor was covered with linoleum, as brown as the walls, but the stairs and landing had carpet, narrow and worn down to the strings in places but still enabling Mr Didcot to go soundlessly up to his own quarters on the first floor. He paused here for a moment, then entered the front bedroom and from the bottom of a chest of drawers extracted an old travelling rug and from the wardrobe, with its fretted top and mirrored door, the long-skirted navy-blue greatcoat he had worn as an air raid warden. Humping them over his arm, he went out again, pursed his lips a little, then turned the key in the door not of his own but of the back room and put it in his pocket.

The stairs up to the attic were of bare and dusty boards. The air was dusty too, for no one ever came up here and there was a smell of mouldy wood which strengthened as Mr Didcot opened the door and edged in. Among the stacked detritus of the past he found the concertinaed shape of the camp bed and putting down his bundle, pulled it towards him. Luckily there was a bit of space in which it could be opened, and he tugged at its rusty hinges until it creaked open, creased and greyly green like a caterpillar. He squeezed round it to the window; it had been closed for years and as he pulled at it the sashcord broke, which at least solved the problem of how to air the room. A child's cot was heaped with newspapers and from beneath them he pulled its mattress and laid it on the bed; it was only half-size, so he took some of the newspapers that were not too dusty and made up the bottom half with them. He folded the rug lengthwise and put the overcoat across it, then stood to consider what more was needed. Pursing his lips, he looked about him, saw and put beneath the bed a child's chipped chamberpot. The air questing in from the window was already bringing its own life with it. Satisfied, Mr Didcot went downstairs again.

His wife stood by the stove waiting for the kettle to boil for a hot water-bottle, watching the youth chew feebly at some baked beans she had heated for him. Mr Didcot stood and watched too; watched the movement of his throat as he swallowed, his long fingers round the cup, his long legs under the table; watched him hold the hot water-bottle she had filled against his flat chest and accept a cushion from her chair; watched him up the stairs, hanging on to the banisters with a long black hand, and up into the attic, almost twilit now. He stood just inside the doorway and watched as he took off the lumberjacket and then the T-shirt. The dark arms were half lost in the dusk, the vest showing pale. He watched as, hesitating, the youth turned his back and unzipped his jeans, stepping out of them and swiftly into the bed, which gave a creak and a shudder.

'There you are then, snug as a bug in a rug. You'll be all right there. Now swallow this down, there's a good lad.' He held out two aspirins in the palm of his hand, a cup of water in the other; watched the thin arm come from beneath the overcoat, the teeth gleam, the throat gulp down the liquid. 'That's right. Now you go right off to sleep till the morning.'

He pulled the coat up round the dark head, tucking the skirts in neatly under the newspapers and blanket.

'There's no need for you to go downstairs again, not for nothing. There's an article under the bed and I want you staying up here right till the morning, see? Mrs Didcot's not to be bothered and I'm going out. I go out every evening, I'm on call round at the hospital, see, I give them my time every evening. So we don't want to hear so much as a squeak from you till the morning, understood?'

In the dimness the young man nodded. His head was round and black against the faded pink of the cushion, his eyes just visible.

Mr Didcot smiled. 'That's a good lad.' He tucked in the coat collar against the neat ear. 'Well, sleep tight, make sure the bugs don't bite.' He closed the door behind him and, treading softly on the bare boards, went about his business.

TWO

Scholars Town High Street is broad and full of movement, beaded with traffic lights, tinselled with fluorescent lighting, seething with housewives with pushchairs and head-scarves, thunderous with buses and huge tarpaulined lorries headed for the M1. There is an Underground, an Odeon, five betting shops and as many pubs, a Bingo hall that used to belong to the British Legion and which opens at six o'clock Thursday, Friday and Saturday evenings; it may be hired for private parties and receptions. Some of the smaller shops have Greek or Indian names, often written up in their own script, and there is a Polish pastrycook whose croissants are as good as any in London.

Behind the High Road lie street upon street of modest terrace houses, with here and there a small square of grass behind railings whose gate is always open for the children who shriek in and out after school to the swings and see-saws, the concrete climbing frame set on the asphalt, and the dogs and cats who industriously dig and water the earth under the laurel bushes. The houses here are flat faced, flat topped, grey brick with painted eyebrows over their windows and a fringe of painted coping along the top like a humble architectural Queen Alexandra. Some of them are coming up a little; they have pink front doors and a carriage lamp beside it, window boxes, and the walls in front of the basement windows have been taken away. Some of them are going down and await development; pale corrugated iron masks their doors and lower windows, their paths are cracked, their gates gone, rubbish is scattered among the sour grass of their gardens, and even to the topmost floor someone has broken their windows.

Behind them, in flattened wastes enclosed by wire fences, rough grass and weeds, three tombstones rear eighteen storeys to the sky, biscuit-coloured, pocked with windows, toothed with balconies, centrally heated, all electric, some of them already inhabited. They share a car park like an inverted swimming-pool; a launderette and a television hire firm will soon occupy the two shop premises at its corner. Nelly Didcot's mother was born in one of the cottages that used to stand here, and all of them had earth closets in their yards.

Other terraces are of gabled red brick, with ornamental scrollwork and leaded stained glass in their front door panels, red and cream tiled paths. They have an air of great respectability but behind the privet hedges dustbins sag and sometimes a motor-cycle swathed in a plastic sheet. The grass of their front gardens has been concreted over, although sometimes there still remains an overgrown hydrangea, some greyish michaelmas daisies or some golden rod. They have survived the Blitz with nothing worse than some ceilings down and some windows out and some of them still have Anderson shelters in the small back gardens, humped with haphazard rockeries where nasturtiums and London Pride and weeds straggle. Behind the prim red brick and coloured glass façades a slow erosion has cracked the walls, sagged hinges, blistered paint; where once one family lived there are now four or five, clusters of Indians who keep their curtains drawn all day, old age pensioners heating soup on gas rings, Irish labourers and shop girls far from home.

But it is still respectable. Windows are seldom opened, adamant against curiosity and the buses that go hurtling past towards the High Street. Children from the nearby Primary school drop lolly sticks and sweet papers along the low brick walls that buttress the privet, swing on such gates as are still swingable, and in the covering dark of winter rattle the letter-boxes and ring the bells, squealing away in anonymity. Bus tickets and empty cigarette packets blow along the gutters.

Arthur and Nelly Didcot live in such a house.

Mr Didcot turns briskly into the High Street and makes for Mansfield's Stores. There is no one in it save two girls chatting behind the counter, for it is only nine o'clock, and the manager in a cubbyhole at the back, walled with ledgers and tins of floor polish.

'Mr Abbott? My name's Didcot, Arthur Didcot. I live round Wardlow Road.'

'Yes?'

'You got a young chap working for you.'

Mr Abbott looked sour. 'I did have. He hasn't turned up this morning.'

'That's what I come about. He's queer.'

'Queer?'

'That's right. Shocking cough and a temperature, even after a night's sleep.'

'He didn't look too good yesterday. Where is he, then?'

'At our place. We can spare him a bed for a night or two till he's better, for you couldn't turn a dog out, the condition he's in.'

'Flu, is it?'

'Very likely. He was worried about his job, see.'

'That's a change. Young fellows you get nowadays don't think twice about going off sick.'

'That's why I come round. I got up the usual time, made myself a cup of tea, thought That's funny, he's not up yet, he'll be late for business. So I give him a few more minutes and then I went up, see, and there he was laying there like a log, fast asleep still and sort of snorting. So I give him a shake, wakey-wakey, rise and shine, and as soon as he opened his eyes I could see he was still queer. He put his clothes on and come downstairs but as soon as I saw him I knew he'd never make it. Sweating and shaking, weak as a kitten, didn't hardly seem to know where he was. So I said You go back to bed, I said, and sweat it out of you. Then he started a carry-on about getting to business and I said Don't you worry about that, I said, I'll pop round and explain, I said, and here I am.'

'Well, that's very kind of you, Mr – er . . .'

'Didcot.'

'Mr Didcot. He seemed a good worker and that's rare enough these days, God knows. D'you think he'll be fit tomorrow?'

'I wouldn't like to say. If he stays in bed today with the aspirins we've given him he ought to be better by morning, but as to coming back to business . . .' He pursed his lips doubtfully.

'It's getting on to the end of the week. Saturday's our busy day. I don't want to be short-handed on Saturday and then find I've got to get someone new to start again on the Monday.'

'Leave it to me, Mr Abbott. We'll get him on his feet again by Saturday. He's keen, see, he doesn't want to let you down.'

'Well . . .'

'Today's early closing, isn't it, so that gives us a bit of a breather. Say he's on his feet tomorrow, he'll be back to work on Saturday, you take it from me. If he's not, I'll come round and let you know and you can make arrangements according. That's fair enough, eh?'

'Well . . .'

'Decent young chaps don't grow on trees these days, you said so yourself. It's not many lads as'd worry at not being fit to come to work. It surprised me, I must say, especially him being what he is.'

The shop is rather busier now and Mr Abbott's gaze moves beyond the neat figure in front of him, in its mackintosh and cap, to the two assistants and their customers. One of them has a toddler with her and you have to watch toddlers.

'Very well, sir, we'll leave it like that. But if he doesn't turn up on Saturday I'm afraid he'll have to have his cards.'

'Understood, understood. He'll appreciate your kindness. Now I can see you're busy so I'll be on my way. But I believe he left his gear here overnight, I said I'd fetch it for him. Kind of a hold-all he said it was.'

'That's very irregular . . .'

'He give me a note so you can check my bona fides.' Smiling, he gropes in his breast pocket and brings out a piece of paper on which is neatly written 'Please hand to Bearer my personal effects' and in a different and uncertain hand, 'Signed E. Winston.'

The hold-all is found at the bottom of the cupboard where the staff hang their coats. It is not large and a seam has split at one corner. Pausing only to buy some Oxo cubes, Mr Didcot leaves the shop and walks home.

He let himself into the house, quietly as usual, for his wife would not yet be awake. Hanging his cap and raincoat on the hall stand, he took the hold-all into the kitchen and set it on the table, then filled the kettle and lit the gas under it, turned on the radio but got the Five to Ten hymn so turned it off again, then settled to the hold-all. He unpacked it carefully, laying each object on the table. There was not very much: a clean but creased white shirt, a pair of ragged pants, two pairs of socks, a pair of shoes that needed mending; a safety razor and tooth brush rolled up together in a plastic bag with a wafer of soap; two copies of *Beano*, one of *TV Fun*, much worn; and, at the bottom, a few photographs and papers. Mr Didcot made the tea and sat down to these.

There was a tinselled birthday card inscribed:

'Loving Wishes Errol from your Auntie Lucille.' There was a programme of a football match played at Wolverhampton three years before with scrawled signatures on it, and an autographed postcard of Shirley Bassey. There was an enlarged snapshot of a family group taken in what looked like a park, for there was a bench in the background; they were all smiling, save a toddler in a frilled bonnet – a stout, pretty woman, two men, a teenage girl with a large white collar to her dress, two schoolboys, the smaller of them almost extinguished by his Cub cap and scarf. There was a coloured postcard of a BOAC Constellation but the date over the Jamaican stamp was illegible. It was addressed to Mr Errol Winston at a street in Wolverhampton and inscribed: 'Landed OK, plane bang full, food OK, Paul was sick! ! Great welcome but wow! it's hot! Mum says will write soon as will your loving Cousin Emmeline.' But there were no other letters.

While Mr Didcot was studying this his wife pushed open the door and lumbered in. She wore the same clothes as the day before. He looked up. 'Morning, Mother. Rise and shine.'

She saw the hold-all. 'What you got there?'

'It's young Errol's.'

'Young who?'

'His name's Errol – our young chap.'

She stared. 'He's never not gone?'

'Couldn't. Weak as a kitten. He's upstairs, fast asleep still, if I'm any judge.'

She sank down on a chair. 'Oh Arthur, is he bad?'

'Not bad but not good enough to go to work. He

come down early and give it a try but I sent him right back again. I bin to the Stores and saw the manager. That's his things. I've had a look at them.'

'Oh Arthur, you shouldn't.'

'We want to know who we've got, don't we?'

Mrs Didcot heaved herself up and leaned forward to see better. 'Poor boy, he hasn't got much, has he? No pyjamas! You'd better lend him a pair of yours, Dad, while he's poorly.'

He pursed his lips.

'Old ones, dear, that you'd not wear again. He can't just lie there in his underwear.'

'We'll see.' He held out the photograph. 'I reckon this is his family.'

She took it. 'Well I never, just look at them! Is that his mum? She's got a sweet face. And the kiddies – aren't they sweet!'

He took the picture back from her and began repacking the case. 'They're willing to keep his job open for him till Saturday, that we do know.'

'Well, I'm sure he's a nice young lad, dear, you can see he's got a nice family.'

'You can't see nothing of the kind, Mother. You can't go by people's faces.'

'Now Dad!'

'You're a real soft touch, you are. It's a good thing one of us has got a head on their shoulders.'

'Get along with you.' She smiled and got to her feet. 'It was you said he could stay.'

'Well, I'm not inhuman. And he took my fancy somehow, I never bin real close to one of them before.

I'll go up and see how he is.'

The attic was full of light for the terraced houses of Wardlow Road were not high and the uncurtained window faced plenty of sky. The camp bed stood clear of the surrounding clutter and on it Errol lay like a roll of carpet. His eyes flashed open as Mr Didcot edged in.

'Well son, how you feeling?'

'Okay.'

'That's good.' He moved forward and set a cup of tea down on the floor, then put his palm on Errol's forehead. 'Still got a bit of a temperature. You stay where you are for today and sleep it out.'

'What did the guvnor say?'

Mr Didcot told him. 'So all you've got to worry about is being fit enough to turn up there Saturday, right? I brought your bag.' He set it down by the bed.

'Thanks.'

'You just lay there and drink your tea. You can have a read of the paper when Mother's done with it. She can't get up here herself, see, because of her legs.'

'That's bad.'

'Yes. So I'll have to look after you till you're on your feet again.'

'The cough's better.'

'That's because of a good night's sleep in the warm. Shall I fill up your hot water-bottle?'

'Okay.' He fished about beneath the coverings and brought out the tepid rubber bag. Mr Didcot watched him, studying the bony brown arms and shoulders against the white of the singlet, the neat small head. In the bright light the skin seemed less grey than it had earlier although the eyeballs were yellow. 'If you need to go downstairs to the toilet you can cover yourself with the coat. Mother's about on the ground floor, so you want to be decent.'

'Okay.'

'Drink your tea, don't let it get cold. D'you fancy something to eat?' Errol shook his head. 'Well – I'll be up again before long.' With a last, considering look he went out, cradling the hot water-bottle like a flabby breast.

All day Mr Didcot tended Errol, going up to the attic every hour or so. Often the boy was asleep and then Mr Didcot would stand in the doorway and regard him carefully, taking in, in meticulous detail, the peculiarities of his alien physical being. Once he came near and bent so close over the bed to examine the wiry hair that Errol woke up. For a moment they stared at each other, almost eye to eye, frozen; then both recoiled, Errol against the old pink cushion, Mr Didcot upright with a smile and a soothing word. At teatime he made the Oxo and Errol drank it and ate some bread and butter. And presently, wrapped in the ARP greatcoat which came only halfway down his dark shins, he went downstairs and out to the lavatory, watched on his return by Mrs Didcot, who had propped herself in the kitchen doorway to see him pass.

'That's right, dear,' she said. 'Feeling better, are you?'

His eyes gleamed in the gloom of the passage. 'I

reckon so.'

'Don't take cold, now. Is your bottle hot?'

'It's okay.'

'Mind how you go, then.'

She watched him up the stairs, marvelling at the pale soles of his feet. Fancy! When her husband went up later Errol was propped up on one elbow reading *TV Fun*. The hold-all, unzipped, stood on the floor by the bed.

'Feeling better, are you?'

'I reckon so.'

'That's good. Nothing like twenty-four hours in bed to put you on your feet again. Is there anything you fancy?'

'I could fancy some milk.'

'I'll see what we can do.'

Errol drank the whole half pint that Mr Didcot had to go out and buy from the milk machine round the corner. By then it was getting dark.

'We shall have to fix you up with a light bulb now we've turned this into a guest room. There should be one somewhere.'

Errol finished the milk, his throat stretched, then wiped his mouth with his hand. 'That'd be great.'

'But you get to sleep again now, eh? Tomorrow we'll have you on your feet.'

Next day he was certainly better. He went back to sleep after drinking the tea that Mr Didcot brought up to him first thing, but while Mrs Didcot was moving slowly about the kitchen in preparation for their mid-day meal, the door was pushed open and there he was, dressed in the T-shirt and jeans.

'Well I never!' she said, clapping her hand to her avalanching bosom. 'There you are then. You give me a start, standing there.'

'He said to come down, the gentleman. When I felt ready.'

'Mr Didcot, dear. We're Mr and Mrs Didcot, like I told you that first evening.'

He smiled. 'I don't remember much about that evening.'

'I daresay you don't, dear. My word, you was queer! Standing there like a poor drowned rat, and cough! I thought you'd cough your heart up. You better now, then?'

'My head feels a bit queer.'

'And no wonder, laying there twenty-four hours and no proper food in you. Sit down, dear. I daresay your legs feel a bit queer too. You timed it just right, for Dad's gone round to the fish shop to get our dinner. We always have fish on a Friday; I like to keep up the old customs.'

'I don't want . . .'

'Nonsense, dear, there'll be plenty.'

He was sitting by the gas fire with an old cardigan of Nelly's round his shoulders when Mr Didcot returned, and managed to eat half a portion of fried skate and chips. They watched him closely, as though he were some rare but domesticated creature whose ways were marvellous. When Mr Didcot went out for his evening duty Errol stayed on for a while in the kitchen, listening to the radio and to Mrs Didcot's rambling talk until it and the heat of the gas fire set his head nodding on the thin neck and she sent him up to bed.

Saturday he was well enough to go to work. Mr Didcot fried him some bread and made a pot of strong tea, and insisted on walking as far as the High Street with him. He stood on the corner and watched him walk away down the pavement towards the Stores, legs long under the hunched black lumberjacket.

'All right, was he?' she asked when she was up and had come into the kitchen.

'Right as rain.'

'That's good. Poor young fellow.'

He came back looking grey again and soon went upstairs to bed. They heard him coughing. 'He'll be all right,' said Mr Didcot before he went out, as usual, for the evening. But when Nelly went to bed that night she stood for a while at the bottom of the stairs, holding on to the banisters, listening. There was absolute silence. Shaking her head, she withdrew to her own room, to unpeel her clothes, haul herself into the bed, re-read an old copy of *Woman*, take her pill, and sink down to the muddy bottom of sleep.

All Sunday he slept, coming down only once to visit the lavatory, consuming only the tea and milk that Mr Didcot carried up to the attic every now and then. Apart from questions about his food they did not discuss him but pursued their normal separate rituals as though they were not both aware of a breathing life up there under the roof where for so long there had been nothing.

When Nelly appeared in the kitchen on Monday she asked at once, 'Is he up?'

'Up and gone to work.'

'Is he all right?'

'Right as rain. We was wise to leave him be all yesterday, he's slept it right out of his system.'

'Well, that's a blessing.' She made her way round the table to her own chair while he poured her a cup of tea. As she sugared it he drew a coin from his waistcoat pocket and pushed it towards her.

'He give me this.'

She peered. 'Ten shillings? Whatever for?'

'His board and lodging.'

'Well I never! What a nice thought!'

'Of course, it's only fair. But I must say I was surprised. You don't get many young chaps nowadays prepared to pay their way without being asked. I must say I was very favourably impressed.'

'You didn't ought to've taken it . . .'

'No, no, fair is fair. He's bin here a week, after all.'

'But he hasn't ate much.'

'It's the principle.' He took the coin back and replaced it in his waistcoat.

She sipped her tea, looking at him over the rim of the cup. 'Why don't we keep him, dear?'

'Well now, Mother . . .' He leaned back, pursing his lips, balancing on the back legs of the chair. 'That's quite a tall order.'

'Go on, Dad, you know you like him.'

'It's not whether I like him or dislike him. I must say he's what you might call intriguing.'

'Have you noticed his ears? He's got lovely ears, just like little brown shells.'

He smiled. 'I can't say I've noticed his ears. It's his hands I've noticed, them big flat nails and then that sort of shrimp colour underneath. Weird really.'

'He can't help his colour, dear.'

'I wasn't implying he could.' He rose and began to put the dirty crockery in the sink.

Tactfully she waited a moment, then said, 'I'm sure he'd like to stay.'

'But I'm not so sure I want him. I've always said I wouldn't have nobody, haven't I? If we'd wanted a lodger we could have had one any day of the week – crying out for accommodation people are nowadays, what with the housing shortage and overcrowding and high prices . . .'

'But he wouldn't be like a real lodger, Dad. I mean, it wouldn't be permanent – just till he got properly on his feet again.'

'I've always prized our privacy.'

'You wouldn't hardly know he was here dear – at business all day and you out every evening. And I'm sure he wouldn't want a proper room or nothing like that. We could just let him clear up the attic a little, and give him a couple of sheets. I mean, he wouldn't expect nothing grand.'

'He wouldn't get nothing grand.'

'Go on, dear, you know you like him.'

He wiped his hands carefully on the roller towel beside the sink. 'He's under the weather now. How do we know what he'll be like when he's fit again?

Drugs, women, all night parties . . .'

'Oh Dad! You can tell he's a nice boy.'

'You're too trusting, Mother.' He patted her fat shoulder as he went to the door. 'You'd welcome all the world, you would.'

She folded her hands in her wide lap. 'It'd be company for me in the evenings.'

'He wouldn't be in in the evenings.'

'I think he would, dear, a young boy all on his own like that.'

'We'll have to see.'

So Errol stayed. 'Just for the time being,' Mr Didcot said, looking sternly at him across the kitchen table that evening as though he were a headmaster moving a doubtful scholar into a class a little too high for him. Errol looked back as though he accepted the role.

'You'd like to stay, wouldn't you, dear?' Mrs Didcot asked.

He turned his mild eyes to her. 'I don't have nowhere else to go.'

'You understand it'd be just temporary. We don't need a lodger, you understand, we've never fancied having a stranger in the house . . .'

'He's not a stranger!'

Her husband quelled her. '. . . and it has to be clearly understood we'll tolerate no noise nor disorderly behaviour nor any monkey business of any description. Your place will be in the attic and down here in the kitchen for meals and a bit of a chat with Mrs Didcot of an evening if she so desires and you happen to be at home. There'll be no intrusion into our personal affairs and if there's the least bit of trouble, you're out.'

'Oh Dad!'

'It's best to get these things clear from the start. I'm sure Errol appreciates that.'

He nodded. 'Okay.'

'Two pounds a week and your supper – and no liberties, see? We've never had no one else in the house and we wouldn't be doing it now if we wasn't sorry for you.'

'How's your cough, dear? Is it better?'

'Yes, it's better. It come on again a bit when I was sweeping the shop and hauling the cases, but most of the time it's better.'

'So what d'you say, son? D'you want to stay? Just for the time being?'

'Okay. I'd be glad.'

So it was settled.

THREE

Errol slid into life at Wardlow Road like a dark foot into a slipper. He came back quietly from work each evening, ate his supper, helped clear the dirty crockery into the sink, then sat listening to the radio with Nelly. After the ten o'clock news they both went to bed. Sundays he slept; he had a great capacity for sleep, which Nelly ascribed to his having been ill and, she was sure, neglected before he came to them. She heaped his plate at suppertime and he ate it all, neatly, quickly, like a cat, wiping the gravy up with a piece of bread in his upturning pink fingers. Soon he ceased to look fragile and grey. A glow came up under his skin and beneath it the bones were delicate but strong. He washed a lot – stripped to the waist at the sink in the mornings while Mr Didcot made the tea, and in the attic after work, carrying a saucepanful of hot water upstairs and bringing the basin carefully down to empty in the lavatory. On Thursdays, early closing day, he went to the public baths and to the launderette, and his two shirts were ironed by Nelly along with her husband's. At the end of his second week he bought some socks and another T-shirt, in which he went to work.

He and Mr Didcot cleared the attic a little and made it more habitable. They stacked things on top of each other along one wall and put the camp bed along the other, made up with some old sheets and the cushion stuffed into a pillowcase, the ARP coat and some frayed and moth-eaten rugs Nelly had disinterred from the chest of drawers in her room. An orange-box covered with a traycloth stood beside it, carrying Errol's comics; and the basin in which he took his nightly wash, with soap and his other toilet things in a saucer, stood on an upended trunk with an American cloth mat to protect it. It was a child's mat, cracked and peeling at the edges, with Humpty-Dumpty grinning from the top of a wall and the verse written out below. His few clothes hung on hooks on the back of the door, his lumberjacket on the shoulders of a dressmaker's dummy. He had drawing-pinned the picture of his family and the postcards of Shirley Bassey and the aeroplane above the bed.

Mr Didcot lingered. 'Fine looking girl, that Shirley Bassey.' She was wearing a lowcut white dress, with her head and neck thrown back. 'Course, she's had a bit of a chequered career. Not surprising, really, show business and all. At least she's more decent than some of them pop groups. This your family?'

'That's right.'

'Mum and Dad, eh?'

'No. My auntie and her kids.'

'No parents of your own, then?'

'Not now.'

'I don't want to pry, you know.'

'That's all right.'

'If there's one thing I value, it's privacy. Me and Mrs Didcot, we keep ourselves to ourselves and always have. And while we're about it, son, let's have one thing quite clear.' He regarded Errol severely from his rather pop eyes. 'No one but me goes into my rooms on the floor below. There's to be no loitering or hanging about on the landing, just straight up here and down again, see? I've got valuable documents in that back room – my Den, I call it – and I'm frequently engaged on highly concentrated studies in there. I sometimes work far into the night. I can't have any interference or hanging about on the landing.'

Errol looked bewildered. 'Why would I want to do that, Mr Didcot?'

'Well no, I don't reckon you would. But it's best to make the position clear right from the start. Mind you, there's nothing there that'd be of any value to an ordinary person. But there's archives there that are worth their weight in gold to them as has eyes to draw the right conclusions. It's a vast project I'm engaged in, I can tell you – a vast project.'

'Is that a fact?'

'It is a fact, son – a solemn fact. That's one reason why we've never taken no lodgers. I can't rightly think how we come to take you, Mrs Didcot's soft heart and my soft head, I suppose.' He smiled and Errol smiled back, causing Mr Didcot to ponder yet again for an instant on the exceeding whiteness of his teeth. 'One day,' he said, 'if all goes well, I might just conceivably give you an outline of what I've set out to do. Only might, mind you. Even Mrs Didcot doesn't know the real vastness of it all. Women can't take in that sort of thing. And she never comes upstairs, see, on account of her legs.'

Nelly's legs were the reason why she never went beyond the walls of the house. Two sticks stood in a corner of the kitchen but she seldom used them, preferring to hand herself from one piece of furniture to the next, the places polished dark by the oils of her stout palms. If the weather were very warm – and a few weeks after Errol moved in, it was – she would push one of the kitchen chairs to the back door and sit there for a while, with a view over the Anderson shelter to some old rambler roses covering the back garden fence, the camomile, dandelions and loosestrife, michaelmas daisies that nothing could kill. Also of the lavatory door, which did not fit very well.

'Why don't you sit out in the front?' said Errol, coming home on early closing day. 'I'll fetch your chair out for you.'

'No thank you, dear, it's too exposed. People see you sitting out the front; they can see you're handicapped and they start interfering. Once they think you're helpless, you can't keep them away. The people that side wouldn't, they're a houseful of blacks – oh I'm sorry, dear, I didn't mean it that way, and they're not none of your lot anyway, they're Pakistanis – but there's an old girl lives the other side you'd never see the last of once you let her over the doorstep.'

'You could sit out of sight, right up behind the hedge.'

'Then I'd be in the dustbin, dear, like a load of old rubbish.'

'That's right.' He grinned, and she reached up and

patted his arm.

'You're a saucy boy.'

Errol and she had grown easy together. He was not a talkative youth but under the soft flow of Nelly's chat every evening he had relaxed. Supper over, Mr Didcot gone to his nightly duties, they sat one on either side of the gas fire and Nelly talked. She liked a good play on the wireless and light music (but none of that pop) and was in permanent mourning for Housewives' Choice and Mrs Dale's Diary ('Not them last ones they had, I couldn't take to them, but them first ones they had for years and years, real friends they seemed like, and the Doctor had such a lovely kind voice . . .'). Telly she and Mr Didcot had never fancied; such an outlay and all for a load of rubbish – crooners and all that sex and nothing but killing and riots on the News. Before Errol came she had turned the radio on every evening as soon as her husband left until the chimes of Big Ben at ten o'clock, and bedtime, her pill, a read of *Woman*, and sleep. Now she turned it on, from habit, but talked through it.

Whether he listened or not was hard to tell, for he sat without moving, his long limbs stretched out, his head drooping a little on the slender neck. There was the flash of an eyeball or of his teeth when he smiled, breaking the fine-boned mask into the face of a responsive boy, so that, one evening, suddenly, the tears came up in her eyes and began to run down and plop on the mounds and folds of her bosom. She groped for a handkerchief among the cushions (which hid so many varied conveniences of her living), smiling at Errol's anxious look.

'You okay, Mrs Didcot?'

'Yes, yes, I'm all right. It was suddenly – seeing you sitting there, you seemed like our Terry.'

'Terry?'

'Terry – our son. He'd've bin older than you, I suppose, but somehow I always imagine him young. Not the age he was when he went but your age, in his young manhood.' She wiped her face, but smiling to reassure him.

'He went away?'

'He died, dear. Such a bright little chap, he was. He would have been fifteen the week after.'

'That's hard.'

'It was silly really. He went up on the Heath with some friends, just boys larking about like they do, and they was climbing some trees – which they're not supposed to do – and the branch broke. A big old elm tree it was, rotten, you know, you can't tell. They took him in hospital but he never knew us. Five days, it was.' She wiped her eyes again and stuffed the handkerchief back among the cushions.

He leaned forward, clasping his fingers between his spread knees. 'My mum died when I was twelve.'

'Oh you poor boy!'

'My auntie had me. She and Mum were close, see, and she had kids and things and my grannie lived with them till she died. My dad too.'

'Is that them in the photo?'

'You seen that?'

She flushed. 'Mr Didcot told me.'

'I'll fetch it down and show you.' He jumped up and hurried from the room, swinging his narrow hips to avoid the furniture, a long dark arrow of eagerness. She sighed and clasped her hands in her lap, staring into the orange bones of the gas fire. Soon he was back, hitching his chair closer to hers.

'That's my auntie, see – Auntie Lucille. And that's her husband, Uncle Flint – that's a family name, Flint, Flint Baker he is. And that's the children – Emmeline, Paul, Hobart and little Janice. They're great kids.'

'And who's that?'

'That's my dad.' He leaned back, his face closing.

'What happened to him, then?'

'He went off.'

'And left you with your auntie?'

'They wasn't here then. They was back in Kingston.'

'Well, that's not far, dear.'

'Kingston, Jamaica. That's far enough, I reckon.' He grinned again, taking the picture back from her and smoothing it with one long finger. 'They bin gone two years now.'

'Why didn't they take you with them?'

'Man, it costs! Besides, there was my dad, he hadn't got no one then. He said we should stay together. Then later he run off. Maybe he's inside.'

'Inside? You never don't mean . . .?'

He shrugged. 'Who knows. He hadn't got much sense. When he'd bin gone a few months I come to London, see what it's like. It ain't much.'

'How long you bin here, then?'

'I dunno – February, March, sometime back.

There's more work here. I was on the Underground first – that's murder. The public – push past you like you was pigs, like you wasn't human. "Move forward please" you have to shout every blessed time, you'd think they'd have learned by now, but not them. And they glare at you like you was an animal.'

'We was down in the Tube in the Blitz. Every night Dad used to take us down there, me and Terry – he was only a toddler then – tuck us up in our bunk and then off he'd go to the ARP. We never saw him again till morning, and very often we didn't know if we'd even do that, what with the bombs and all, but he never had more than a scratch. Course, it wasn't too bad round here, not like some places, the East End and that. And we had a lovely crowd down there, all friendly together, and laugh! And sometimes, when it was really coming down outside, we'd have a bit of a singsong. "Run rabbit" we used to sing, and "There'll always be an England" . . . Oh, we had some fun down there and no mistake.' They sat in silence for a while, oblivious to a discussion on the Common Market which the radio had been having for the last ten minutes. 'So what did you do then, dear?'

'This and that. I was on street cleaning for a bit. I reckon that's where I got that cough.'

'You want to take care, dear. At least you don't smoke.'

He grinned. 'No, I don't smoke – not nothing.'

'Mr Didcot wouldn't have had you if you smoked. He's a very clean-living man, dear, he don't hold with smoking nor drinking nor nothing like that. He was brought up very strict. And then him working in the hospital, seeing what people bring theirselves to... He feels strongly. He gives his services free there every evening now, after working there all those years. After the ARP, that was.' She paused for a moment. 'I shouldn't tell him about your dad, dear, if I was you. You know, about where he might be. He's funny sometimes.'

'Okay.'

Except first thing in the morning and on Sundays Errol and Mr Didcot hardly saw each other, and even on Sundays, not very much, for Errol slept till midday. On weekday mornings there was little exchange between them, for Errol was taciturn beneath Mr Didcot's chat, washing at the sink while the talk flowed on and Mr Didcot's gaze took in unwaveringly the smooth brown contours of his torso. He drank his tea without sitting down, watching the clock, and was quickly gone.

'You ought to give yourself more time,' Mr Didcot would say, sitting in his shirtsleeves over a plate of fried bread and tomato. 'You'll give yourself a gastric condition, never sitting down to a proper breakfast.' Errol would smile and gulp down the rest of the tea, his throat stretched and the Adam's apple rolling like a smooth brown ball in its column of muscle, set down the cup, wipe his mouth with the back of his hand, say, 'Thanks, Mr Didcot, see you' and go, leaving his host to shake his head and begin on the day's immutable routine.

Mr Didcot was neat as a cat, and when he had

finished his breakfast he washed up all the dirty crockery that had been dumped in the sink and on the draining-board since last night, wiped down the table and the gas cooker, and made fresh tea for his wife's arrival. 'Morning, Mother, rise and shine' he would say, and hauling herself round the table she would answer, 'Morning, Dad, is there any tea in the pot?' and they would sit and drink it together and listen to the Morning Story on the radio.

Then, while she made herself some breakfast, he would take a dustpan and brush and do down the stairs, or perhaps venture on her bedroom (just to sweep, no sense in trying to tidy), then go upstairs to set his own domain in perfect order yet again: neat narrow bed, bare surfaces, a wardrobe, little else. Upstairs again, now that Errol lived there, to make sure he'd left the attic as it should be, to leave a clean sheet and pillowcase alternate Mondays, and to pry a little. There was not much he didn't already know: new comics now and then and, over the weeks, a new shirt or socks or pair of pants, neatly disposed in polythene bags on a cleared shelf of the bookcase. The bed with its hotchpotch of bedclothes, the orange-box and trunk used as a washstand, made a neat clearing in the jungle of attic furniture. When Errol had been there three weeks Mr Didcot took a mat that had been outside the door of his bedroom and put it beside Errol's bed; it was cosier than bare boards.

When Mr Didcot's housework was done, he went to the shops. Fish fingers and four bananas, a sliced loaf and a quarter of a pound of tea – his purchases were all small, for the routine he had chosen was one that took him out of the house and into the High Street every morning, rain or shine. He varied his marketing, familiar at most of the shops but known to none; only at the newsagent at the corner was he a regular, buying the *Daily Mail* each morning and, once a year, a birthday card for Nelly.

Three or four mornings a week he went on to the Public Libary, to gather a pile of reference books and spread them out on the big table, put note pad and ball-pen ready and, lips pursed, peruse the pages, taking notes, referring from book to book, a small concentrated figure beside the African students and the old people around him.

Back at home again, shopping unpacked, he sat and read out items from the newspaper to Nelly while she made their lunch, listened to The World at One and disputed with those speakers with whose views he disagreed. After lunch Nelly dozed in her chair through Woman's Hour and the afternoon play and Mr Didcot went upstairs and shut himself into his Den till teatime.

Soon after six Errol returned; Nelly called 'Is that you, dear?' and he called back that it was, going upstairs two silent stairs at a time. Presently he came down again to empty the basin down the lavatory, appearing eventually in the kitchen, clean and crisp and quiet. 'Well I don't know, Mother,' Mr Didcot often said in the first weeks, 'I always heard them darkies were happy, laughing creatures, singing and carrying on all the time. But Errol – you'd hardly know he was there.'

'He talks a bit in the evenings.'

'Does he? Well, he never talks to me, hardly opens his mouth.'

'I think he's in awe of you, dear.'

'In awe of me? Get away!' But he was pleased.

Supper over, during which he discoursed on topics of the day, Mr Didcot washed and brushed himself, put on his jacket, folded his mackintosh over his arm, took his cap from the hall stand, said, 'Well, no rest for the weary' and left the house. He never returned until Nelly was in bed and asleep with her pill, and Errol too asleep, long and limp and unconscious – for sometimes Mr Didcot crept up to the attic to see. He would stand in the darkness with the door eased open, his sight adjusting until, peering round, he could make out in the light of the street lamps Errol's shape in the camp bed. There would be no sound but that of their separate breathing, Errol snoring quietly, regularly, oblivious as a child, Mr Didcot shallow and faster, wheezing a little; and outside the occasional car whisking by – it was too late for buses. He would close the door gently and go carefully down the bare stairs, shut himself into his bedroom and undress in the dark (for the street lights shone brighter here), put on his striped winceyette pyjamas and button them to the neck, and lie down in his iron bed and after a while close his eyes.

Sometimes he did his marketing at Mansfield's Stores, stretching his neck discreetly to peer into the back of the shop for a sight of Errol, but only once did he see him, dressed to his ankles in a sand-coloured overall and unpacking a carton of detergent. 'What d'you get up to at business, son?' he asked from time to time. 'What sort of jobs do they give you?'

'All sorts. Anything. Sweeping the store, unpacking – anything.'

'Do they give you any responsibility now you've bin there a while?'

'Sometimes Mr Abbot lets me help with the orders.'

'That's good, that's good. You want to try and move yourself up a bit, look ahead. You don't want to be sweeping floors all your life. You can aim a bit higher than that.'

Every Friday evening Errol handed over two pounds for his rent. Mr Didcot took it, checked it, folded it away carefully in the wallet which he kept in his waistcoat pocket. 'What you doing with the rest of it, son?' he asked one day when Errol had been with them over a month.

'Now, Dad!' Nelly was shocked.

'Errol don't mind me asking, do you, Errol? It's concern rather than curiosity.'

'I don't know, Mr Didcot. Saving it, I reckon.'

'That's good. That's very sound. What you saving it for?'

'Clothes, things like that. I'd like a real sharp suit.'

'You'll need a good warm overcoat when the cold weather comes,' said Nelly. 'We don't want you getting that cough again.'

'That's true, that's very true, son. You take her advice, you need to take care of that chest of yours.'

'I reckoned maybe,' his face was bright, 'maybe I'd get one of them sheepskin coats, you know, with the fur inside.'

'That'd be nice. You'd look nice in brown.'

'Tell you what – if it's a nice day Sunday we'll go up the High Street and have a look in the shop windows. There's not much I don't know about the shops round here and you don't want to go throwing your money away.'

Sunday was fine, a high blowy day forecasting autumn, and just before teatime Mr Didcot called Errol softly and together they left the house, Nelly still asleep in the kitchen. The streets were quiet; discarded bus tickets rustled as they blew along the pavement to lodge in corners or twine in the privet hedges, and empty ice-cream cartons rolled in the gutters. The litter bins on the lamp-posts were stuffed with newspapers greasy from fried fish. Outside the newsagents on the corner the wire rack clanged in the wind and someone had overturned a crate full of dirty milk bottles. Only a couple of dogs, a father with a child in a pushchair, moved in the Sunday stupor.

Mr Didcot walked briskly, two steps to one of Errol's long paces, chatting as they went. 'I like a bit of a walk on a Sunday. Keeps the liver in order and gives Mother a chance for her snooze. Mostly I go the other way, up towards Parliament Hill. Lovely up there it is, on a clear day. I daresay you know it?'

'No, I never bin.'

'Never bin up Parliament Hill? Well, you've a treat in store and no mistake! You ought to go up there one early closing, give yourself some fresh air. Winter or summer, when it's fine I go up there of a Sunday, you never know what you'll see – model boats, football, kiddies' playground, always something going on. I can't hardly remember the last time I come down the High Street of a Sunday. We'll turn left here and cross over.'

They crossed and walked more slowly past the closed shop fronts, the washing-machines, tinned fruits, cabin trunks, First Communion dresses, shirts. At each Men's Outfitters they halted, studied, Mr Didcot discussed. On a suave model they saw just the thing – 'Suede type, that's what you want. My word, it's a price though – murder the way the price of things has gone up. They ought to be hung, charging like that.'

'It's not bad.' Errol shaded his hand against the window and squinted in. 'You got to pay prices like that for decent stuff.'

'My word, you'll have to save up for a month of Sundays to have the money for that.'

Errol smiled. 'That's okay. I don't need nothing else just now.'

Mr Didcot studied him. 'Mind you, you'd pay for dressing. Put you in decent clothes and you'd make some of them long-haired hippies look like savages. I mean it, son. If there's one thing I can't stand it's slovenliness. Show me a slovenly man or woman and I'll show you a slovenly mind. Put you in decent clothes and you'd put them all in the shade, never mind your colour. With those long legs of yours and that slim build, you can wear anything.'

'Thanks.' He turned away and began to move on down the pavement.

Mr Didcot caught up with him. 'Well, you've seen what you want and you know what it's likely to cost you. The only thing is to find the money to pay for it. You want to hold on to that job of yours.'

'That's okay. I like the job okay.'

'And there's one thing I will say for you, you don't go throwing your money away on smoking and hanging round the caffs, like some of the youngsters do these days.' He was getting a little out of breath, for Errol's pace was faster than his. 'Mother tells me you're home every evening.'

'That's right.'

'Don't you have no pals, then?'

'Not here.'

'Wasn't you with friends before you come here? I seem to remember you saying . . .'

'That's right. But they was the other side of London. They moved away.'

'And you moved away too. Why d'you come some where where you didn't know no one?'

'I wanted to see – get away. I didn't like that crowd over there.'

Mr Didcot quickened his pace. 'Wild, were they? Razor slashings, drugs, that sort of thing?' He lowered his voice. 'Pimping?'

'Some. There was all sorts. I like to be quiet.'

'And a good thing too, if you want to be in a respectable household like me and Mrs Didcot's. I wouldn't stand for no wild goings on, I can tell you that. That's one thing I will say for them Pakistanis next door. They're quiet. Wouldn't hardly know they was there. Mind you, their cooking smells something terrible sometimes. Comes right through the wall at you. But live and let live, I always say. If there's one thing I can't stand it's prejudice.'

They halted at traffic lights, Mr Didcot puffing slightly. He eased his thin neck in its collar. 'It's a nice afternoon,' he said. 'Why don't we go up Parliament Hill for an hour or two?'

'Okay.'

'Hop on a bus. That's what the adverts say, isn't it – hop on a bus.'

They hopped on a bus. Mr Didcot insisted on paying, expansively genial to the West Indian conductor and observing with curiosity that between the two young men there passed nothing but indifference. (He mentioned it to Nelly later on, when Errol had gone upstairs. 'Funny, you know, you'd think there'd be kind of a fellow feeling. But no, not a flicker. Less than a couple of dogs passing in the street.'

'Fancy!' said Nelly.)

The wind was dropping and the slopes of the Hill were mellow in the evening sunlight, the trees below its crest dark cumuli beneath the bright clouds that towered across the sky. The tennis courts were vivid with movement and half the tables at the refreshment koisk were still full, the ground littered with lolly sticks and straws.

'Would you like a cup of tea, son?'

'I'd like some milk.'

He tried to pay for it but Mr Didcot waved him away. 'You're saving up for that overcoat, right?'

Errol smiled. 'Right.'

They sat at a puddled table from which, beyond Errol's shoulders, Mr Didcot could see the tennis players darting to and fro. He took off his cap and ran a handkerchief over his forehead, placing his cap on his knee. Opposite him Errol sucked at a straw, eyes downcast above the neat nose and wide lips, concentrated on the drink.

'All right, is it?'

He nodded, eyes flashing upward for a moment.

'That's good. It's nice here. Does you good to get out in the fresh air. There's an outdoor Lido nearby – you ought to try it.'

'They'd let me in?' His smile was sardonic.

'Course they would. We don't have no colour bar here, son, it's a free country. You've got rights just the same as what I have.' Errol said nothing but drained the milk carton with a derisive sound. 'I mean, here I am sitting here with you and no one taking a blame bit of notice. There's every colour of the rainbow here.' He gestured in the sunlight, which lay blandly on bare arms and legs of pink and brown and black, scattered over the green slopes like confetti in thin bright clothes, their children running between them. 'You don't want to get a chip on your shoulder, son. You won't be treated no different from anyone else in this country. Why, I doubt if me and Mrs Didcot would've taken you in if you'd bin one of ourselves. We've never fancied a lodger, but you're – well, you sort of took our fancy.' He stirred his tea and drank it, dabbed his lips with his handkerchief, watching three girls with fat white thighs go sauntering past. 'How'd they treat you at business, then? They treat you right, don't they? How'd the girls treat you? There's two of them, as I recall.'

'Three. They're okay. They're friendly.'

'I bet they are, a nice-looking young chap like you. What do they do, pull your leg? Get up to larks, do they?'

'They're just friendly.'

'You ought to invite one of them up here for a stroll one afternoon while the weather keeps nice. Walk over and look at the ponds – they've model boats there, dozens of them, grown men mucking about in waders just like a lot of kids. And angling. There's plenty to see. Plenty to see in the bushes too, when it gets a bit dusky. But you'd not have nothing to do with that.' He put his cap primly on his head and buttoned his jacket. Looking impersonally into the distance, after a pause he asked, 'D'you know much about girls, son?'

'Some.'

'Ah. Your own kind, were they?'

'My cousins had plenty of friends.'

'I suppose they would have. Easy going, up to all hours, parties... I've always heard you people were more – well, different from the way we look at things. More easy going – common law marriages, that sort of thing.'

'My auntie and her family went to Methodist church

every Sunday of their lives and Sunday school for the kids.'

'Don't get me wrong, Errol. I wasn't implying nothing wrong. I'm sure your auntie and uncle was fine people, they must've bin to bring up a decent young lad like you are.' He reached across and laid his hand on Errol's narrow wrist. 'I wasn't implying nothing wrong.'

Errol said nothing, his face closed.

Mr Didcot gave the wrist a little pat. 'It's just, you never going out of an evening, I wondered if you was shy of girls, see? You don't want to be shy of girls, not at your age. Not so long as you treat them decent. Never do anything that's not nice. But taking them out – a nice walk in the trees, the back row at the pictures, well, that's only natural, seems to me. I mean, a fine-looking young fellow like you, in your prime . . .' His voice faded; then, looking away, he straightened himself and stood up. 'Well, I suppose we'd best be getting back. Mrs Didcot'll be ready for supper.'

Next evening, after Mr Didcot had gone out as usual, Errol, who had been particularly silent, went upstairs and did not reappear for some time. When he did, he had the picture of his family in his hand. He sat down across the hearth from Nelly, who was already settled in her chair, and leaned forward with the photograph between his fingers.

'My auntie – she was okay.'

'What d'you say, dear?' The informative banter of

News Desk had already been switched on.

He raised his voice and repeated, 'My auntie was okay. She was real good. That whole family was real good.'

'Don't put them all in the past, dear. They're still in the land of the living.'

He held the picture out to her, shaking it impatiently until she reached forward to take it. 'You study them faces. They're good faces. Even my father, he's got a good face.'

She studied them and then him. 'Of course they have, dear.'

'My auntie, she run us all, see? She saw to everything. And she'd sing all the time, quiet like. If she wasn't talking she'd be sort of humming to herself. Wherever she was, you knew, see, because she'd be singing. When my mum died, my auntie sang and the tears was pouring down her cheeks. They was close, my mum and my auntie, and my auntie run us all when my mum was ill. She was ill a long time, just laying in bed getting thinner, and my auntie'd come in and cook and clean and see I got to school and my dad got to work and there'd be dinner for us when we come home. And she'd be singing. In church she'd sing and sometimes everyone else'd sort of die away, just listening to my auntie, and then they'd all join in again. It was great. My auntie was great.'

'She's got a lovely face.'

'Yes.' He took the picture back again and studied it. 'Nothing but the best would do for my auntie. She brung us all up like we was kings of England. We wasn't allowed to run wild like most of the kids, we had to behave nice at table, do our homework, keep ourselves nice. She was set on Emmeline being a nurse.'

'That's nice. That's a lovely life, being a nurse.'

'You got to have passes, see, to be a nurse, and Em didn't get enough or something. Me neither. But my auntie, she didn't blow her top nor nothing, she just kept after us so's we got proper jobs, clerking and that, when we left school. I had some good jobs, when I left school. They look after you, see; they've got what they call a Youth Officer or something, sees you get started right. My auntie was dead set on our starting right.'

'You done all right, dear. She must be pleased.'

He put the picture beside him on the table, laying his hand flat over it for a moment. 'She don't know my dad run off.'

News Desk was ended and Nelly leaned over and turned down a documentary on Louis Pasteur. 'Haven't you heard from her, then?'

'She don't know where I am.'

'Well, that's a shame, dear. You being so fond of her and all, why ever don't you drop her a line?'

He shrugged. 'I don't have nothing to say.'

'But you ought to write, dear, she'll be worried to death. Beats me why you didn't go back home with them all.'

'It's not my home. I never bin there.'

'They say home's where the heart is. I should've thought your auntie'd have wanted to keep you all together.'

'She did but my dad wouldn't.'

'That's a shame.'

'He reckoned we'd do all right on our own, the two of us working. He's got a trade, see, he done all right when my auntie was seeing after us. Then after she went, bit by bit he didn't bother no more. Then he went off.'

'That's sad.'

He shrugged again. 'He wasn't much good. He was all right while auntie kept after him. But all he liked after she'd gone was drink and betting. And girls.'

Nelly clicked her tongue, her pouched old face full of concern.

'He wasn't much good,' Errol repeated, taking up the picture and looking at it again. 'But my auntie was okay. She was great. I just wouldn't want no one to think bad things about my auntie.'

'I'm sure no one wouldn't do such a thing.'

'Mr Didcot was saying some things. Yesterday, when we was out.'

'Dad was? I don't believe it!'

'Nothing straight out. But sort of hinting we was all – well, like my dad.'

'I'm sure he never meant no such thing.'

'No, well, I thought I'd better tell you, see, so's you can get it right. I don't like people like my dad, people like what Mr Didcot and that thinks we're all like. I didn't like the lot I was with after I come to London. I like to live decent, like my auntie brung me up. that's why I struck off on my own.'

He got to his feet, looking down at her, shut behind

his blackness.

She struggled forward in her chair. 'I'd like your auntie,' she said, 'I wish you'd write to her. Be a good boy now and write and tell her you're among friends.' She put out a pudgy, rough hand and took one of his where it hung by his side, giving it a little shake. 'Go on now, be a good boy and do what I tell you.'

His cold fingers responded and he smiled. 'You sound like my auntie.'

'I couldn't come up to her, dear, could I? You write to her.'

'Maybe.'

'I'll keep on at you!' They smiled together and let go their hands.

'And you explain to Mr Didcot so he'll get it right, see?'

'Don't you worry, dear. Now sit down again and be cosy.'

'No. I feel itchy. I'll go for a walk round.'

'Take care of yourself, then.'

He took the photograph back upstairs and then went out.

Errol walks in the lamplit streets. The orange glow of the sodium lamps throws hardly any shadow, turns his skin the same dark mauve as the corners and angles of the streets. He walks with his shoulders hunched, hands in the pockets of his jeans, making them tighter than ever on small buttocks, long thighs. The streets are quiet, for it is the dead time between opening and shutting, with everyone snug inside bar parlours, cinemas and Bingo halls, and doors shut tight against a sharpish wind. Soon Errol will need his simulated suede jacket, and he turns in the direction of the shop, out of Wardlow Road, where he has been the only person, into the High Street, where there is some traffic, but flowing gently, slowing quietly at the traffic lights' command where almost nothing crosses now, resting, not surging off on the amber, for at this hour there are no traffic problems, schedules can be kept, everyone is calm, neutralised by the orange-purple lamps.

He walks along the pavement, more slowly now, his attention drawn by the bright shop windows: there are three-piece suites in plastic leather and armchairs shaped like embryos in acid green nylon tweed; a standard lamp with three graded clusters of pink-tinted bulbs; a fur fabric panda three feet high leaning against a simulated teak coffee table with brass legs. There are windows full of blouses and underclothes, crammed as close as hundreds-and-thousands, from the walls, from the ceiling, upside down, sideways, with floating legs displaying pantihose. There are supermarkets, bare aisles lit to their furthest corner, wire baskets stacked, grapefruit and cereal and toilet rolls heaped in the windows beneath posters cross-barred like heraldic bastardy with slashed prices. There is a milk machine outside one of them and Errol buys some, tearing open a corner of the carton with the help of his teeth and drinking it where he stands. There is a litter basket by the bus stop and he puts the empty carton into it, wiping his mouth with his hand.

Beyond there is a Cypriot café, its name written in Kyrillic script, its door and windows closely curtained but lit. Beyond that a photographer's studio full of bridal couples, minily trendy at registry office, maxily white at church, all shapes and colours; babies too, and youths in forage caps and sailor hats, keen. Beyond that a pub, from whose swing doors come Irish voices thick as the warm fug of alcohol and smoke. Two or three men push loudly out and stand disputing amiably, absorbed in themselves; but Errol crosses the empty road and continues on the other side.

Soon here is the gentlemen's outfitters. In the strange light all the smiling dummies look coffee-coloured. Above twill trousers Errol's jacket is thick and masculine, furry collar turned up round plastic ears, plaster hand extended in friendship from the furry cuff. He stands, envisaging. And the tangerine shirt with matching tie; the turquoise turtlenecked Bri-nylon sweater, the kimono-type towelling robe in green and yellow; the suede half-boots; the navy-blue pyjamas. . .

Three or four youths come skylarking round the corner of the crossroads; one of them tries handstands on the railings that guard the kerb, the others pretend to push each other under the wheels of an approaching bus. They are hallooing and laughing, joining in ribald versions of a current song, their boots scraping the pavement as they jostle each other. Errol withdraws into the unlit doorway of the sweetshop next door to his jacket, and waits while they racket past him. When they have gone he comes out again, studies his jacket once more, and walks on.

He is warmer now, more relaxed, walks with his head up and his long arms free. There are other people, a few middle-aged women with carrier bags full of who knows what, gossiping as they walk to the bus stop, a girl or two walking fast, sometimes another coloured man. They see each other but no look passes. Errol walks on. There is an oily smell from the Deep South Fried Chicken shop but it is empty; trade will be brisk when the pubs and cinemas shut. And here is the cinema itself, its vestibule bare of everything save the sweet stall and the ice-cream freezer, its outer walls showing blood dripping from the green jaws of some nameless Thing onto the almost naked breasts of a crazed countess. Next week three hard-riding brothers will be decimating those nineteenth-century opportunists who sought to treat the Redskins as less than brothers.

Errol moves on. The shops are smaller now and soon end altogether, although he is still on the bus route. There are terrace houses of various ages, some with old trees obscuring their windows, leaves drifting to the pavement. Blocks of council flats, balconies bared like teeth and some still bannered with the day's washing, forgotten in the darkness, hedges and grass and chrysanthemum put in by the Council, lamp-posts lighting the courtyards. Small factories and work yards, Glass Cut, Motor Repairs, Wholesale Sanitary Supplies; a fried fish shop, a garage, another pub; new shops, another supermarket, the hot breath of the

Underground, another High Street. He has left Scholars Town; this is a different place.

He walks, waiting to find a main street off to the left which will lead him back to his home. The air is not quite so tranquil now, there are more cars, the doors of cinemas and Bingo halls are being opened and wedged back, the doors of pubs swing to and fro more often. There are more people, more purposeful. On the corner of a turning which seems like the one Errol is looking for the big windows of a café throw their light across the pavement. He walks past it, seeing the chromium and formica, the urns and vats of orangeade, the cabinets of rolls and pies, doughnuts and chocolate biscuits, chewing gum and peanuts, the sauce bottles and cruets and jars of paper napkins, and Mr Didcot sitting in a corner watching the teenagers at another table.

Errol walks on, round the corner, on down a darker street, turns left again; eventually he is in Wardlow Road, the shaggy privet dusting his face as he dodges by. There are people about, going home, in a hurry; buses full of standing room only. Dogs are being let out, cats called in, the pubs loosing a great wave of beery air as their doors are bolted shut. Voices, a song or two, footsteps. Front doors will close, tellies will be switched off, plugs pulled.

Errol lets himself in and goes upstairs to his attic. Nelly's door is shut, she is deep asleep. The landing is silent, its two rooms are empty behind their shut doors. Errol does not know what time Mr Didcot will return nor why he was sitting in that café instead of helping out at the hospital as declared. He wonders about it, but not for long. It is not his habit to speculate on things which have no instant answer.

He sleeps.

FOUR

Sunday became the day when Mr Didcot cultivated Errol. When the weather was fine they walked or took a bus to Parliament Hill; once or twice, when it was not, they saw the four o'clock programme at the cinema, which let them out in time for supper. Mr Didcot liked to sit at the back among the courting couples; with a waggish air he explained, 'When you're a pocket Napoleon like I am it's easier to see round two heads stuck together. Put me behind someone your height, son, and I can't see the blooming screen at all.'

Sometimes, as November advanced and it grew dark earlier, Mr Didcot would suggest refreshment and they would enter one of the few cafés open on a Sunday afternoon, drink a cup of orange-coloured tea and a glass of milk and sometimes put a coin in the juke-box. Mr Didcot tapped on the table with his finger-tips in time with the beat. 'D'you like dancing, Errol?'

'Some. Me and my cousin used to go to the socials sometimes, Christmas and that.'

'You ought to go to the dance halls. I bet you'd set them by the ears there, eh, those long legs of yours. I always heard you people was natural dancers. When I was a young chap there was a dance going called the Black Bottom. What a name, eh? Wasn't no offence meant, you know, it was just a name. We wasn't all so conscious of racial conflict in those days. It's Hitler that started it – old Adolf. A for Adolf, eh?' He regarded Errol speculatively for a moment and was silent for a while.

Presently Errol said, 'Mrs Didcot'll be wondering.'

'What's that? Ah, you're quite right. Mustn't keep supper waiting. There's not much life going on here anyway, this time of a Sunday. You ought to come in one weekday evening, I bet things fairly hum then.'

The following Sunday Mr Didcot was less loquacious than usual over the midday meal. When it was done and Errol had washed up (which had become his weekend task) Mr Didcot drew himself up, buttoned his waistcoat, regarded Errol sternly and said, 'Son, I've come to a decision.'

Both Errol and Nelly, who was propped against the draining-board drying the dishes, stared at him apprehensively, so grave was his tone.

'I've decided to show you my Project.'

Nelly clasped the drying-up cloth. 'Arthur!'

'Yes I have, Mother. He's bin here long enough to warrant my confidence.'

'I'm sure he's done that, dear.' She smiled up at Errol, patting his arm with a thick, rough hand. 'It just wouldn't seem the same without you now and that's a fact.'

'And it's not as though he's likely to try and make something out of it, like one of our own lot might.'

'That's true, dear. Well, you're a lucky boy, Errol, I can tell you. Mr Didcot's never let nobody look at his Project, not all the years he's bin working on it. I've never had a peep at it myself even.'

'That's your legs, Mother. If you could get up the stairs I'd have shown you – although I doubt you'd have understood more than a fraction.' He looked at the clock on the mantlepiece. 'Shall we say in an hour's time, then?'

At half past three Mr Didcot summoned him. He looked approvingly at the clean white shirt into which Errol had changed, the slender neck rising darkly, and a yellow pullover from Marks & Spencer's. He himself was spruce, in a grey alpaca jacket with horn buttons that Errol had never seen before. His eyes were bright and there was a bustling excitement about him as he chose a key from the chain buttoned to his trousers and unlocked the back room door. 'Go on,' he said. He threw out an arm and bowed slightly. 'Enter Aladdin's cave.'

The room was dim. The light of a late winter afternoon hardly penetrated the lace curtains at the window over which were almost drawn heavy drapes of dark red plush. The carpet too was mainly red, a worn but still opulent Turkey which had been inexpertly cut to fit from wall to wall and round the narrow fireplace, where wheezed an old-fashioned gas fire, domed and pinnacled like St Paul's, and a gas ring with a kettle on it. Along the same wall as the fire was a divan, lumpy and low to the ground, covered by an Indian bedspread. A large table stood against the opposite wall, covered in neatly stacked papers, flanked by bookcases; and above them was pinned a variety of charts, graphs and tables, ruled and marked in differently coloured inks. All this was revealed when Mr Didcot nipped ahead of Errol and switched on a lamp on the desk.

'Cosy, isn't it? I bet you never expected to find something like this tucked away up here. There's very few people indeed's bin privileged to peep inside my sanctum.' He looked round proudly, enjoying Errol's astonishment. 'I daresay you're wondering what it's all for. There's not much possibility of your being able to grasp the whole concept, of course. It's too vast, even if you was trained up to it. That's why I've made it so comfy up here. Brain fag, see? An hour or two of concentrated mental energy and I'm like a wet rag. I have to stretch out on the couch there, make myself a cup of Nescaff. And while I'm laying there recuperating some of my best thoughts come to me.'

He moved to the door and closed it, then waved Errol to the divan. 'Sit down, son. Let's make ourselves snug.'

Errol sat gingerly on the edge of the couch, looking about him, hands dangling between his knees. Mr Didcot lit the gas fire, then crossed and drew the heavy curtains over the November murk. The room was lit in chiaroscuro, for the lamp threw light only on the surface at which it was directed, and the gas fire glowed red. Mr Didcot turned the desk chair round to face Errol and sat down, crossing his knees. He studied him benignly and in silence. Then, 'Well, what d'you think of it, eh?'

'It's great.'

'Great. Yes. You've hit the nail on the head there. This little sanctum of mine is totally dedicated to a great project, the discovery of two dominating aspects of civilised man's nature – intellectual power and physical recoupment. After the striving comes the reward. On this wall behind me –' his voice dropped and he made a gesture, laying his hand heavily on a pile of manuscript, 'and in these papers, you see the structure of a whole new concept of historical thought. I don't expect you to be able to understand it, but you might just be able to grasp the outline of it, to dimly perceive what it is I've got hold of. But one thing must be clear.' He became stern. 'What I'm telling you must be in strictest confidence. I want your word of honour on that.'

'Okay.'

'The intrigues and jealousies in the world of scholarship would astonish you. If the least hint of what I'm working on was ever to get out, before I'm ready for publication, that is, it'd be either snapped up and published as somebody else's discovery or sneered at and derided out of pure jealousy. Because I haven't got no so-called academic qualifications. Pure jealousy. The whole scholastic world's riddled with it. So what I try and explain to you must never go beyond these four walls. Understood?'

Errol nodded.

Mr Didcot became benign again. 'Mind you, it's because I know I can trust you I'm telling you all this. I mean, it's not like you was a young chap with a lot of pals and the same sort of background as what I have. I don't rightly expect you'll be able to make head nor tail out of most of what I tell you but –' he paused, 'sometimes the thinker gets lonely. It's lonely work, thinking, specially when it's revolutionary theories you're at work on. Sometimes you just long for an understanding voice, someone you can trust to share your confidences, know what you're after without any argy-bargy. A sort of disciple – a son, maybe.'

Errol opened his lips but shut them again without speaking, glancing about the shadowed walls out of the corners of his eyes without moving his head, spell-bound by Mr Didcot. From where he sat his host was a dark figure against the strong light on the desk behind him, head sunk low on shoulders that sagged a little for a moment. But he soon drew himself erect again.

'It was that that started me off, really, opened out my train of thought. Eighteen years ago, it was. Eighteen years of dawning insight. We called him Terry, see, but his full name was Arthur Terrence, and when he passed away I got to thinking, tracing the significance of the name right back. It's my own name, see, Arthur, and the more I pondered over it the more the theory formed itself, and I came to follow it and see it prove itself right through history.'

The darkness, the heat, and Mr Didcot's absolute conviction suspended all sense of reality and time. His voice went on and on against the hoarse purr of the gas fire and Errol sat motionless, hands dangling between his knees, round-eyed.

The theory was this: There was a mystical power

about the letter A, traceable throughout English history – and perhaps, Mr Didcot was just beginning to surmise, world history. In the beginning was the A, the Alpha, the first letter of the alphabet, the beginning of all things, the letter that began the name of the first man, Adam. A great mystery lay on every bearer of a name beginning with this mystic letter. You had only to look at history, particularly – and this was Mr Didcot's dazzling insight – English history. For who was the first great English king? Arthur. Noble, wise, betrayed, unable to fulfil the knightly promise of his nature yet a symbol down the ages of chivalric purity. What might have been the course of English history had Arthur lived to old age? Must it not be that those men marked with the Alpha bore a special power which nevertheless carried with it a doom of unfulfilment?

Study the concept closely. After Arthur, Alfred. He too a symbol of courage and tenacity, leading his little band of warriors against the fearsome Norsemen. Had he been able to bind the lesser kingdoms to him, what might have happened by the time the Normans landed? Duke William might have been faced with a totally united nation, solid against him, and the Norman French might never have conquered Britain.

Makes you think, doesn't it?

Next little Prince Arthur in the Tower. Must you with hot irons put out both mine eyes? Young boy, I must. And will you? And I will. Well, he didn't, but Arthur was killed just the same. Now that young Arthur was in line to the throne. Supposing he hadn't been done away with?

Another Arthur was King Henry the Seventh's heir, to whom Catherine of Aragon was first married. But he died and his younger brother became king and husband to his brother's wife. And we all know where that led England. If Arthur hadn't died, had reigned as king, had stayed married to Catherine – no divorce, no split with the Pope, a Roman Catholic succession and who knows, perhaps through a male line? The mind reels at the possibilities.

The same thing again with the next Prince Arthur, James the First's eldest son. If he hadn't died in childhood, we'd never have had Charles the First. There'd have been no Cromwell, no Reformation; so no Charles the Second and the shift back to Catholic James Stuart and all that he led to. No house of Hanover.

All Arthurs, all born to the purple, all cut off before they could fulfil their destiny.

There's an Albert next – although Alberts are not quite so powerful in their symbolism. Prince Albert, Queen Victoria's grandson, eldest son of Edward the Seventh and Queen Alexandra, to whom May of Teck was first engaged. Heaven knows what would have happened if he'd lived for he was a bit simple by all accounts. It was probably a good thing he died and Princess May married his brother, sailor George.

Since then there'd been no more important royal As – although it needed to be noted that Edward the Eighth's second name was Albert. Noted, too, the effect Prince Albert had had on English life through his influence on Queen Victoria, although he was not strictly speaking English royalty. Also to be noted that our present Queen's father was christened Albert although George was used when he came to the throne – perhaps someone in high places had already noticed the fatality of royal As, for despite the change he didn't live long, did he, poor chap?

Now there were no more As in line for England's throne – not unless you counted young Prince Andrew, but he was a long way down the line.

The more you studied it, the more complex it became, the more mysterious the significance of A– and in particular Arthur, as though once that noble sovereign had returned to the legends from which he came, the name (or its alternative Alfred) carried within itself its own power which, when unrecognised, brought about drastic changes in the current of history. There were other aspects too, which were now opening up to the mind that had eyes to see: Alexander the Great, for instance, Ataturk, Adolf Hitler. Who knows where the concept might lead, once the initial leap forward had been made, and all of it needing hours of study and research.

'These books, see,' Mr Didcot gestured, 'a reference library I've built up over the years – history, biography, all following my chosen line. That Encyclopaedia – I got that before the war in one of them Free Gift schemes the newspapers was running. Never thought I'd make the use of it I have, not in those days. It's been the basis of my researches, that and the Public Library. I've built up all my reference books from that.

'Then here, up on the wall – genealogical tables, son, complete to the last detail, cousins, infants dead before the age of two, the lot. And graphs showing how the movement goes – direct or bilateral, Salic law and so on. There's a chart there comparing the subjects' development at similar ages, giving a line on how they might have turned out if they'd lived – psychology, that is, and I've got some books on that too. Then here –' he laid his hand on a fat postcard album, one of several stacked on the desk, 'here's portraits of all of them, as well as I can. I've had to do some detective work there, I can tell you – little Arthur in the Tower, now, there's hardly a known likeness anywhere. But you've got to have them, you've got to study their features – physiognomy, that's called – you can read charater from a face, you know.

'And this –' he turned right round from Errol and lifted one of the piles of manuscript, hefting it lovingly, 'this is the Project itself – my life's work, you might call it. Everything I've been telling you now is set down here in black and white in far more detail than you can possibly imagine. I've left not a stone unturned, son, I've proved every one of my findings up to the hilt. There's facts and findings in here that's historical dynamite, that some of them Oxford dons'd give their right arms to get hold of. That's why it's all such a matter of secrecy, why I don't never let no one into my confidence. And the only reason I've done so with you, Errol, is because somehow, you being different and that, not in the same world somehow, I feel I can trust you. I mean, who'd you ever be likely to know that'd be in the same field? Even –' he smiled, 'even if you was able to understand the half of what I've been telling you.'

The cessation of Mr Didcot's voice brought movement back to Errol. He straightened his back, stretched his legs out over the Turkey carpet, blinking.

'Well,' he said, 'that sounds great.'

'That's just what it is – great. It's a great new conception, a rereading of the tides of history. And I've not come to the end of it yet, not by a long chalk.'

'You must've read a lot of books.'

'I have, son, I have.'

'Reading books – I reckon that's really great. You must be – like a schoolteacher or something.'

Mr Didcot chuckled. 'Something a bit more brainy than that. It's vision, see – vision that's needed.'

'The only thing . . .' Errol gazed at him with round eyes, 'I mean, your name being Arthur too and all of them in history not coming to no good . . . I mean, don't it scare you?'

'No, son.' He looked down at his linked hands with an inward-turning smile. 'I'm not scared. There's a power in the name – my whole Project's based on that. But it's only royalty that brings the doom to it. I've just got the power.'

FIVE

Very soon it was Christmas. The weather was muggy and wet and Nelly fussed about Errol's chest, for when it rained he refused to wear the sheepskin jacket (recently achieved) for fear of spoiling it. Mr Didcot had told him he might use the spare umbrella in the hall stand but when Nelly tried to make him take it he had laughed, zipping up his lumberjacket, and said, 'A right nit I'd look, wouldn't I – a big black boy under a big black umbrella!'

Nelly's pouched face went red and she cried, 'Don't you say such nasty things, Errol! You're not black.'

'Well, I'm not pink, eh?'

'You're lovely. I won't have you saying such nasty things. As though it made any difference . . .'

So he took the umbrella sometimes, if it were raining hard, but more often went with the collar of the lumberjacket turned up under his neat ears and the rain dusting his close head like frost. 'Oh, you are a bad boy, Errol!' Nelly would cry when he came home, hoisting herself out of her chair indignantly, 'I don't know what we're going to do with you. Look at your jacket – soaked through. Where's that umbrella Dad give you? And change those shoes this minute!'

Laughing, Errol wiped the rain off his head and face, sat down and unlaced his shoes obediently.

'You go upstairs now and change your socks. Go on now, do what I tell you. We don't want you down with flu again, do we, you bad boy.'

'Yes, Ma, right away, Ma.' Grinning, he padded out in his stockinged feet and she, wheezing, would bend laboriously down to pick up his sodden shoes and set them on the fender near the fire.

A few days before Christmas he brought back a glittering small tree made out of green plastic. 'My auntie always had a tree – bigger than this, and all silver. She hung sweets on it, Polos and Smarties and that, for us kids.'

Nelly rummaged about in the cupboards and drawers of her bedroom and retrieved some tinsel string and stars, tarnished gold now rather than silver, and some dusty paperchains. Errol looped them up with drawing-pins, specially bought, transforming the kitchen into a kind of marquee. He had worked late at the store each evening of that week and as a reward was given a box of crackers and some crystallised fruit, for which there would be little market in the New Year. The Store closed early on Christmas Eve and when he got home he sat with Nelly and listened to the King's College choir on the radio.

'My auntie ought to hear that.'

Nelly wiped her eyes. 'It's lovely, really lovely – like angels.'

'We used to go to carol services – all hymns and that and some of them old spirituals. It was more cheerful than this lot.'

On Christmas Day he produced a huge flat box of

chocolates with a red satin bow and a picture of a thatched cottage on the lid; and Nelly gave him two pairs of underpants which her husband had agreed to buy from Marks & Spencer's. And she had laid two packets of Smarties under the branches of the tree. There were no Christmas cards, for none of them knew anyone.

'What a shame your auntie don't know where you are. Did you write to her like I said?' He shook his head. 'Oh, you are a bad boy! She'll be worrying. I've a good mind to write to her myself.'

'Finish your dinner, Mother. We don't want to be eating for the Queen.'

Mr Didcot had watched the festive preparations with indulgence, joked about the paperchains, admired the tree, had pulled a cracker or two and read out all the riddles, and for a few minutes consented to wear a paper hat with the others. He had explained to Errol that Christmas was so much superstition on to which commercial interests had fastened for the exploitation of the public. He and Nelly had not bothered with it for years; exchanging presents was a waste of money. All they had done for a long time had been to roast a chicken or a nice piece of pork, get a plum pudding from the grocer's, and listen to the Queen and the rest of the holiday broadcasts. 'Of course, it's different if you have kiddies. The kiddies like it.' He smiled at Errol, 'I reckon you must be a bit of a kid yourself, the way you've got the kitchen festooned and that.'

But once Christmas Day was over and the catalepsy of Boxing Day, and life, however shaky, had been restored to the streets, Mr Didcot's eyes sharpened. Before and during the holiday he had sat back benignly while Nelly and Errol amused themselves, and had observed the comfortable to and fro of their communication. He had invited Errol into his Den again and showed him one of the albums of royal portraits, sitting next to him on the divan with the album open across their two sets of knees; but he had drawn nothing like the easy, open response that Nelly got. He had watched Errol's long fingers pointing over the pages, his absorbed downcast face, and answered his respectful questions in a kindly way that he could understand. But Errol did not smile with him as he did with Nelly, he was not natural and free; he was too much in awe.

Soon after New Year's day, as Errol was leaving for work, Mr Didcot said, 'I'm going to give you a treat this evening, son. I'm going to give you an evening Up West.'

'Up West?'

'That's right. A look at the bright lights. You get back sharp from business, put on your best bib and tucker, and we'll give ourselves a night out.'

They take the Underground, emerging from the warm gales of the tunnels into the gusts of a cold January evening. Errol turns up the collar of his sheepskin jacket and Mr Didcot tightens the muffler at his throat, sets his cap more firmly on his head. 'Let's have a bit of a walk round first,' he says, 'and then a bite to eat.'

The Square is as brightly lit as a ballroom, the night sky miles above out of sight. People of every description seethe or stand about, in queues for the cinemas or staring at the blazing lights, in the porches of shops where a young guitarist picks out a few notes or an old man wheezes from a violin. Powerful wafts of frying oil gust on the wind, from a hamburger stall in a side street and from the restaurants before whose windowed menus people stand in doubt. The garden is closed, pigeons and a statue motionless at its centre; the public lavatories are not.

They walk round the pavements, Errol hunched but tall, Mr Didcot to his shoulder, taking neat steps. They choose a café and sit down on the plastic wood and plastic leather seats, choose fried food from a huge plastic menu. All the waiters are coloured, from the pale honey of Hongkong through the Indian continent to the darkness of Nigeria, cooking waffles in the big window. Mr Didcot chuckles. 'I feel like a foreigner,' he says. 'Go on, don't stint yourself. Have a Knickerbocker Glory.' He himself ends with a cup of tea but watches indulgently while Errol spoons up the sweet goo. It is warm in here, and that and the food and pleasure have brought a shine to Errol's skin that catches the orange light, showing up the planes and hollows of his bone structure, delicate under the smooth flesh.

'I used to bring my boy Up West for a treat on his birthday. When's your birthday, Errol?'

'July.'

'We shall have to come back here again then, shan't

we, give you another treat. Of course, he was only a lad, he liked Madame Tussaud's and that sort of thing. You ever bin to Madame Tussaud's?' Errol shakes his head. 'Well, you've got a treat in store then. We'll make that our next port of call. You can study some of the subjects I've been telling you of there – you know, in the Project.' He winks and Errol smiles back uncertainly. 'You never bin about London much?'

'No.'

'Why's that?'

'I only knew them friends of my dad. They was in Brixton, I never seemed to go no further than that. There was a bunch of them – they never mixed with no one else. Some of them was crazy ...'

'You got a lot to see, then – Madame Tussaud's, the Houses of Parliament, Soho . . . I bet you never bin to Soho?'

Soho is also ablaze with light but the night sky presses down lower, lying on the roofs of the houses. Smells are different – hot fat but with alien things frying in it. Music roars from narrow doorways and lights wink and run over life-sized photographs of girls with fans and painted nipples. Errol's eyes grow round, Mr Didcot peers from beneath the peak of his cap, lips pursed. 'Disgusting. Worse than Paris, it is now. You ever bin in one of these places?' Errol shakes his head, gulping. 'And if you're wise you never will. It's easy enough to imagine what goes on – disgusting. I don't know why it's allowed.' The nipples and haunches multiply, music throbs. A man in a red tuxedo invites them in. Mr Didcot pulls Errol away.

But there are more.

They pause at a shop window. From behind protective wire mesh magazines and books display themselves: *Queer*, *Leather Living*, *The Way of the Whip*, *Boy;* three lilac-tinted women bare their teeth at each other from a tangle of limbs and tasselled sofa cushions; two young persons encased in black leather fondle a motorcycle; the *Khama Sutra* looks drab.

'Worse than the Continent,' hisses Mr Didcot. 'You'd think people had something better to do.'

'Want to look around, guv?'

Errol pulls Mr Didcot away.

The side streets are darker, lights coming from basements or from the draped windows of expensive restaurants. Cars parked solid on each side of the roadway hem the pedestrians to the narrow pavement studded with parking meters. There are warehouses, alleys, closed shops; front doors open on to passages, a light on the landing upstairs, white slips of names by the bell push. The beat of music. Lights again. More strip...

As they walk down the silence of Wardlow Road, their footsteps sharp on the pavement, the wind making their eyes water, Mr Didcot says, 'I hope this evening hasn't given you ideas.'

'Ideas?'

'Well, I don't suppose you never saw nothing like some of them nude posters before. White girls.' Errol says nothing. 'I mean, I wouldn't have took you if I'd thought it'd give you ideas. It was just a night out, see? Give you some fun. You don't have much fun, do you, for a young chap.'

'I do okay.'

'That's one of the things I like about you. You're quiet. You keep your own counsel. Like me. But you need some fun too, a young chap your age. As long as it's nice. I wouldn't want you to do nothing that wasn't nice.'

They are nearly home.

'Course, you got to be careful too – I mean, white girls. Wouldn't do, would it? You ought to meet some of your own kind. Have some fun. You ever get in any trouble, son, you come and tell me.'

They turn in through the bushy privet and Mr Didcot takes out his key. The door opens silently on the dark hall; Nelly's door is shut, her light out. 'Shh!' whispers Mr Didcot. In the silence a snore comes gently, and again.

Mr Didcot grins, winks, takes off his cap and raincoat, unfolds his scarf, hangs them all neatly on their pegs. They tiptoe upstairs with never a creak. On the landing, under the weak light, Mr Didcot lays his hand on Errol's arm, looking up at him softly.

'All right, are you?'

'Sure.'

'Maybe I shouldn't have let you see them posters. We won't mention them to Mother, eh?'

Errol shakes his head.

'Still, a young chap like you – you need to know what's what, eh?'

'I'm okay, Mr Didcot. It was great.'

He gives Errol's arm a little squeeze. 'We'll do it

again, son, eh? Give you another treat. Well, sweet dreams . . .'

He watches Errol go up to the attic, turns off the light, goes into his room, and the door shuts on darkness.

The attic was dark, lit only by the lamps outside in the street, from which there came no sound.

It was the dead middle of the night, some few days after the Soho outing. Since then Mr Didcot had been thoughtful yet restive, seeming to burn with some inward hidden flame that lit his eyes but revealed nothing. Now, fully dressed in the middle of the night, he bent over Errol, shaking him awake. 'Errol – Errol – wake up, son. Rouse yourself.'

He stirred, turned on his back, staring up blearily into Mr Didcot's face.

'Get up, son. Come on now, wake up.'

'What is it? What's up?'

'Ssh now – keep your voice down.'

He reared up on his elbow. 'What's up? Is she ill?'

Mr Didcot's teeth smiled in the darkness. 'She's as right as rain, asleep and snug as a bug in a rug. Get up, son. Don't trouble to put on a coat, it's warm downstairs.'

Errol threw back the bedclothes, set his feet on the floor and slowly stood up, hitching his pyjama trousers round him. The placket fell open and he adjusted it, staring bewildered at Mr Didcot, who laid his hand on Errol's arm. His grip was fierce.

'Come with me, son. I've got something to show

you. Quietly, now.'

Still grasping Errol's arm, he led him out and down the stairs. The door to the Den was ajar and the dim orange light of the lamp showed round the rim. Mr Didcot put a finger to his lips, peeping mischievously up at Errol as he pushed the door open and Errol through it. In the black and orange shadows Errol peered about, while behind him Mr Didcot stepped inside and closed the door.

'There,' he said, 'over there.'

Errol looked towards the divan. 'Jesus Christ!' he whispered.

Mr Didcot said complacently, 'I thought that'd surprise you.'

On her back, one leg trailing to the ground, lay the body of a woman, young at first glance, in mini skirt and boots, fair hair cropped round a thin face. She was bundled up in a coat of shabby fur a little shorter than her skirt, from which her spindle legs and arms trailed, the hands grubby and bearing huge rings of metal and glass. Her mouth sagged open and she snored.

Errol turned his eyes on Mr Didcot. 'Is she stoned?'

'Stoned? Drunk, d'you mean? Well . . .' he pursed his lips, 'just a little. She wasn't feeling well . . .'

'She take something? Is she high?'

'High.' Mr Didcot considered. 'She may have taken something. She's certainly flat out.'

Errol took a few steps towards her, peering down. Her greasy blue eyelids were shut; apart from the snoring, she might have been dead. 'Where you find her?'

Mr Didcot joined him, rubbing his hands together. 'Just by the bus stop. She was hanging on to it, looking ever so queer. Hullo young lady, I said, are you all right? and she just looked at me in a pitiful sort of way. My word, I said, you do look queer, where d'you live, I said, and she just shook her head and I see she hasn't got no handbag nor nothing, and the last bus has gone, so I get her arm over my shoulders and I says Hold hard, young lady, you'd better come home with me for a bit till we get this sorted out, and I get her inside and up the stairs and she passes out.'

'What you going to do with her?'

'Well, I thought we might undress her. Take her coat off, I mean, get her a bit more comfortable.' He bent down and lifted the coat away. A pink sweater, not very clean, showed flattened breasts. 'Come on, son, lend a hand. You take her shoulders – inside, that's right.'

Gingerly Errol slid his hands inside the coat and pulled her up. Her head lolled forward and she uttered a loud snort. Mr Didcot peeled the coat from her arms and pulled it from underneath her.

'That's right. Lay her back now.' Errol did so. 'Out like a light, isn't she. Best get her boots off. Go on.' He watched while Errol hesitatingly lifted the girl's foot from the bed and pulled. Her body jerked but the boot stayed on, and Mr Didcot came and held her knee. 'Give it a good tug, now. Don't play about.' The boot came off and the thin leg flopped back on the Indian bedspread. 'Now the other one.' Errol bent to the foot on the floor, seized it and tugged. Mr Didcot held the other knee. 'Keep your eyes on the job, son. We don't want to take advantage, do we?' Holding the boot, Errol stared at him. 'I bet you've never done this before, eh? Taken off a young lady's clothing while she couldn't say nothing. Not a white young lady, anyway. Maybe you never had the chance with one of your own sort neither. Learning something, are you?'

Errol pulled the boot off and stepped back. Mr Didcot retained the knee for the moment, then let it go. The leg fell back on the floor, splayed from the hips.

Errol spoke hoarsely. 'What you going to do?'

Mr Didcot pursed his lips again. 'Best let her sleep it off. We'll make sure she's out of here first thing in the morning before Mother's about. We don't want Mother to see her, that'd never do. Put her on the first bus. I've done it before.

'You have?'

'Certainly, son, certainly. Not often, mind you. I mean, not even I'd do it often. Trash they are really, silly kids. No homes, no families, no moral standards. I mean, look at her.'

They looked down at her, spread on the couch like a grubby puppet. Apart from her eyelids, she wore no makeup; her skin was coarse and sallow, with pimples round the mouth, half open from narrow teeth, a pallid lipstick almost all slopped off. Her hair, dark at the roots, stood in spikes over her ears and brow, roughcut like a boy's. Her nose stood up sharp, like a small beak. Her breasts sagged sideways from her ribs, which rose and fell, rose and fell with her snores, and her thin

pelvis was like a basin. Her legs splayed open from it.
'Best put her legs together, son,' said Mr Didcot primly, 'it's not nice her laying like that.' Errol took a step back. 'Nervous, are you?' He laughed indulgently. 'There's nothing you need worry about. She's out for the count.' He lifted her leg and laid it beside the other on the divan, smoothing upwards. 'These tights! Silly, if you ask me. Spring a ladder and there's a whole pair down the drain. What it must cost them!' He stood looking down at her. The room was hot, for the gas fire was full on, and both men were sweating. 'Look at her,' mused Mr Didcot. 'She don't look much, does she? Wandering about the streets all night half drunk, sitting in caffs waiting for something to happen. There's too many of them, Errol, there's too many lost kids like this one. They're lucky to run across someone like me who'll take them in for the night, get them off the streets. You don't know what could happen to a girl like this, left on her own all night. You ever seen a pair of tights, son?' Errol shook his head.
'They're an ingenious invention.' He bent down and delicately folded the small skirt back over her stomach. Under the close-fitting mesh her pubic hair was bunched. 'I wouldn't mind having shares in tight manufacturing, when you consider the wastage. They're elasticised, see, right the way up, fit nice and snug. Care to slip your fingers inside, son?' Errol made a strange sound and took another step back. 'No need to be nervous,' said Mr Didcot abstractedly, 'she's out for the count. Course, it wouldn't do if it was just you and her on your own, specially her being white. But

it's all right with me here, I stand in what they call loco parentis. As long as I'm here it's all right, you can do what you like. Satisfy your curiosity.'

From a choked throat Errol said, 'What you going to do?'

'I'm not going to do anything, son. I'm just going to sit here beside her till she wakes up. Then we'll both help her to leave.'

He shook his head violently. 'Not me.'

'Now Errol . . .'

He made for the door, hunching his pyjama trousers awkwardly before him. 'Not me.'

Mr Didcot put out a hand. 'But son – I don't think I can manage now without you . . .'

'You got her here, you get her out.' He threw open the door and plunged out. In desolation Mr Didcot heard him rush the stairs, the attic door slam. On the divan the girl gave a great gurgling snort and flopped more comfortably onto her side.

Errol went straight out next morning, without his breakfast and without going into the kitchen at all. At supper that evening he hardly spoke, although Mr Didcot was quite chatty. After Mr Didcot had put on his cap and raincoat and gone off as usual for the evening, Errol said, 'Ma – I got to leave.'

'Leave, dear? What, leave the Stores?'

'No. Leave here.'

'Leave here? Whatever for?'

He stared at her helplessly and she stared back.

'Aren't you comfy upstairs, then? Dad said you'd

made it ever so comfy. You say if there's something you want, dear, and we'll see about getting it.' He shook his head. 'Why d'you want to leave, then? Are you moving in with friends?'

'No.'

'I know that's what young people like to do, move in with friends. Stands to reason, really, it's a lot more fun being with your own age instead of an old couple like Dad and me. I can understand it. But you won't get the looking after . . .'

'That's not it.'

'Then why, dear?' He shook his head again. 'Where'd you go? You haven't found nowhere?'

He twisted his hands, staring down at them miserably. 'I just feel – I got to move.'

'But why, dear? Where to?' She heaved herself forward in her chair and reached out to lay a rough, puffy hand on his knee. It trembled slightly. 'I know it's not very grand but me and Dad's done our best to make you feel one of the family. That's what we've come to think of you as, dear – one of the family. You know that, don't you?'

He nodded.

'Then what you want to go and leave for? You say if there's something wrong and we'll try and put it right. Is your room all right? If only I could get these poor old legs of mine to get me up those stairs to see for myself . . .'

'No, no – you mustn't come upstairs!'

'I could try, dear. Women see more of comfort than men.'

'No. The room's okay.'

'Errol.' Her hand pressed down on his knee. 'Errol, look at me, dear.' He raised his head and looked at her. Her pouched old face was young with tenderness and grief, her eyes were full of tears. 'Errol, I don't want you to go. You've brought a bit of brightness into the house. If you was to leave – well, I don't know how I'd bear with it now. If there was a reason – if you was getting married or something – well, I'd just have to grin and bear it. But just for the sake of moving on . . .' She shook her head and the tears spilled.

'Ah don't, Ma . . .'

'I'm a juggins, that's what I am.' She released his knee and felt for a handkerchief amid the cushions and shawls of the chair. He pulled one from his jeans pocket and thrust it at her. 'Thanks, dear.' She smiled, wiping her eyes. 'I bet you wouldn't have one of them in your pocket if you was living on your own. I see after you, don't I?'

'You bin good to me. It's not that.'

'We bin good to each other. Having you in the house, it's livened us up – more like when my Terry was here. Like we was a proper family.' She blew her nose. 'Don't go, Errol.'

For a moment there was silence. Then, 'Okay,' he said.

Joy came up in her face like a surprise. 'Give us a kiss, dear.'

He slid off the chair on to his knees beside her and she put her arms round him. She smelled stale and warm and he sank into her softness. She kissed him and pressed his head against her cheek. 'That's a good boy.'

They stayed quietly together for a while, then she said, 'My – don't your hair feel funny – like lovely soft wire wool.' She held him away. 'You don't mind me saying that, do you, dear?'

'I don't mind.'

'Weird and wonderful, that's what you are, dear – weird and wonderful.'

'Like black is beautiful. That's what some of them say, the lot I come away from – black is beautiful.'

'Well, some is, dear. Like anything else. You are. You're a lovely boy, Errol. And you'll stay with your old Ma?'

He shut his eyes and nodded.

Two mornings later, as he came down the stairs to go straight out to work, Mr Didcot came to the kitchen door. 'I want a word with you, Errol.'

He stood the other side of the table, in shirt sleeves and unbuttoned waistcoat, pale and stern. 'You upset Mother very much the other evening, talking about leaving. You've upset me too. There was no call to go on like that, after all we've done for you.' His eyes were cold, his mouth pursed as he regarded Errol standing awkwardly in the doorway. 'I don't know where you think you'd go. There's trouble enough finding accommodation without having your disadvantage. I should think you'd know when you're well off, living here like one of the family. Mrs Didcot's got very atttached to you. You upset her, talking like that. Haven't you nothing to say for yourself?'

'I didn't mean to upset her . . .'

'Well, you did. You upset me too. I don't like ingratitude. Me and Mrs Didcot took you in like a stray cat and we've done our best for you. I've given you my confidence, tried to give you a glimpse of the vast scope of the Project. I don't expect to have you turn round and talk about leaving. You wouldn't find many people ready to take someone with your disadvantages into their hearth and home, as you very well know. You've had experience of that, haven't you, before you come to us, living from hand to mouth, drifting from place to place like a vagrant – you, with a good family background behind you – you ought to be ashamed. Your auntie'd never hold up her head again if she knew you was giving up a good home like this to live off the streets again.'

'I never done that.'

'Near to it, my boy, near to it, I'll be bound. I know what you young chaps are like once you tear up your roots. I seen dozens of 'em hanging about the street corners and in the caffs, up to any old mischief, drugs, thieving, pimping – no wonder the police take a hard line with you lot, they've got their work cut out keeping this country decent. Once one of you lot makes a mistake he's on the slippery slope, I can tell you. But when he's living in a decent place like this is, with decent people like me and Mrs Didcot ready to vouch for him, well, he won't have no trouble. Because he won't *be* in no trouble, see? You need to get your priorities right, son.'

He glared at Errol. Colour had come up in his cheeks and the tip of his sharp nose. 'So we'll have no more talk about leaving, eh – that is, not if you've any sense of pride in yourself, let alone consideration for others. I don't expect Mr Abbott at the Stores'd feel quite the same about employing a fellow who walked out on the decent people who'd taken him in and given him a respectable background. I don't think he'd feel quite the same at all. Living hand to mouth it's hard to be trustworthy.'

'He give me the job before I was here with you.'

'Ah, but he didn't know that, did he?' Errol was silent. Mr Didcot softened a little. 'You'd better make up your mind which side your bread's buttered. You're on to a good thing here with me and Mother, I tell you frankly – and I tell you frankly we'd be very sorry to see you go. Of course, it isn't all roses for us by any means. There's the extra cooking and having a stranger in the house, misunderstanding one's actions now and again . . .' His grey eyes stared straight into Errol's. 'But we'd miss you if you was gone. You're something different.'

They stayed without moving for a moment, Mr Didcot fixing his gaze on Errol as though to force his acquiescence, Errol hangdog and confused. Then Mr Didcot turned away, took a covered plate from the stove and pushed it across the table.

'I fried you an egg. Go on, sit down and eat it.'

Errol sat down and ate.

Their blameless Sunday walks and occasional

cinemas were resumed. Mr Didcot was as blandly talkative as ever, but Errol more silent. Even with Nelly he was less talkative than he had been, sitting with her in front of the gas fire while the radio sang and spoke, his hands limp, his eyes downcast, so that sometimes she leaned across and touched his knee, saying, 'Wake up, dozey, we're not dead yet' and he would stir and smile and say 'I heard you, Ma.' But often now, as the days got longer, he would go out after supper, when Mr Didcot had departed for his occupation. He was never gone for long, usually returning before Nelly went to bed after the News at ten, to help her to her room and take her whiskery kiss on his cheek and go upstairs to the attic, quickly past the locked door of the Den, to the bed which his body knew and sank into, straight to sleep.

'Going out, are you?' Nelly would say as he shrugged on his jacket. 'That's right, dear, you be with your friends.'

But he had no friends. He walked about the streets and fell into the habit of calling in for a coke and a bag of crisps at a café where most of the customers were the same colour as himself. Some of the older ones were from the West Indies but most were English-born and spoke with London accents, their native tastes and temperaments adjusted to the English streets, their characters pressed out between the spicey hugger-mugger of parental home and the bare boards and asphalt of their Primary school. Their voices were high and sweet, despite the accent, and they made a good deal of noise just talking. There was a juke-box and sometimes some of them would stand up from the hard chairs and start to dance, but that was soon stopped by the proprietor. 'You wanta dance, mate, you go to the club, see?' But most of them had been to the club while still at school, had battered the ping-pong table and the aged record-player and the well-meaning people who ran it, and had drifted away from it as they had drifted away from the hopeful jobs the school Youth Employment officer found for them – for it was easy to find a job as office boy or van boy or putting things in bags at the cash desk of supermarkets when you were fifteen and eager and clean; not so easy to climb upwards at seventeen and eighteen, with higher rates of pay and the rough discipline of school dropping away. Now they made their own society. A few white youths used the café too – the owner was a Pole – but never brought their girls. The two groups were friendly but kept to their own tables; and when they burst, bored, out onto the pavements, they did so separately.

To sit at a table, drink a coke, listen to the jukebox and chat idly to youths of his own generation was all Errol did. When the noise got too loud or the horseplay too rough he would either leave quietly or close in on himself till the roisterers roared out into the street. There they soon quietened, became wary, drifted away in twos and threes. Only a few stayed skylarking, voices pitched high, eyes sharp and militant for the fuzz or the Paki-bashers. Some of them lit cigarettes that didn't smell quite right, shielding the butts in their cupped hands. A few went on to clubs the Youth

Club couldn't compete with, in basement rooms thick with savoury smoke and smells, furious music and fierce talk. Mostly they drifted along the pavements to lean against the railings at the crossroads, test the slot machines in the shop doorways, kick the empty ice cream cartons down the gutter and slowly separate. Some never went home all night, slept all day; most of them, like Errol, went home along the dark side streets and let themselves into houses where no one cared very much. Several times, when he had been living the other side of London with his father's friends, he had been stopped by policemen and asked to show the contents of whatever bag he carried, turn out his pockets; once, with an angry friend, he had landed in the police station for a while. These incidents had taught him silence and wariness, and so at night he walked quickly, close to the walls, glad to reach home and Nelly filling her hot water-bottle, the close smell of old food and carpet and gas fires.

'Had a nice time, did you?' she'd say, and he'd answer 'It was okay.' Once she said, 'You ought to bring some of your friends back here one evening, give them a cup of tea. They'd be welcome.'

'They're not that friends, Ma. We just meet in the caff. They're wild, mostly.'

She patted his hand. 'You're a real loner, dear. That's what they call them, don't they – loners?'

'That's right.' He grinned. 'I don't belong nowhere.'

'You belong here, dear, and don't you forget it. It was ever so lonely before you come.'

SIX

It was April, juicy and turbulent, buds showing too soon, great clouds swinging across the sky. Mr Didcot had taken him to walk on Parliament Hill on Easter Sunday, had viewed the shrouded roundabouts and other apparatus of the fair nearby and given his views on the undesirability of this ancient saturnalia, the rowdiness and obscene behaviour it brought forth and left under every bush. 'Skinheads and hippies,' he declared. 'A proper jungle they turn it into. You want to steer clear, son. You're just about their mark. You take my advice and don't go nowhere near the Heath tomorrow.'

Errol didn't. He slept late, walked round the empty streets alone, listened to the radio with Nelly after Mr Didcot had gone for the evening, and went to bed early. Deep, deep asleep, he dreamed that Didcot was clawing him back to life once more, shaking and whispering him into the silent darkness of the small hours, the cold house, the shadowed attic, Mr Didcot's head looming huge and close as he bent over him.

'Errol, Errol – wake up. Wake up, boy.'

'What?' He reared up, shrank back.

'Wake up. Get up.'

'No.'

'You've got to.'

'No.'

'You've got to!' He threw back the covers and dragged at Errol's arm, his fingers digging into the flesh.

'Leave me alone.'

'You do as I say!' He was ferocious. In the dusk from the street lamps his eyes were brilliant, his forehead filmed with sweat. 'Get up, I tell you. Get up and come downstairs.'

'I won't.'

'You will. You've got to.' He tugged so hard that to save himself from falling onto the floor Errol put his feet out.

'Come on, come on!' He could hardly stand still, his face working, his hands pushing Errol towards the door.

'I don't want to – not another one . . .'

'It's not like that. Go on, get moving.' He pushed Errol out of the room and followed closely down the stairs. The door of the Den was open, throwing a ruddy light out onto the landing. Errol hung back, clutching his pyjamas, but Mr Didcot gave him another push and he half fell through the door, Mr Didcot following quickly and shutting it behind him.

As before, the room was hot, the gas fire hoarse, the light red and black over walls and ceiling. As before, on the divan lay a girl. A fat girl. And this time her eyes as well as her mouth were open.

Mr Didcot could not stay still. His fingers felt and fiddled over his mouth, his collar, his hair, while he stared with pop eyes at the sprawled figure on the couch. 'I don't know what happened,' he said, 'I simply do not know what happened. One minute she was right as rain, the next...'

'What you done?'

'I haven't done nothing. One minute she was right as rain, the next she – she give a sort of gurgle...'

'You done something. You must've done something.'

'I tell you I didn't do nothing!'

'How'd she get here, then?'

Mr Didcot moved restlessly. 'Well – you know. I was up on the Heath, the fair. We got talking. I give her a couple of cokes. She'd got nowhere to go...'

'You brung her here like the last one. She passed out like the last one.'

'Not like the last one. There was nothing wrong with the last one. She went home right as rain when she'd slept it off.'

'But this one's dead!' His voice rose and Mr Didcot cut in sharply.

'Keep your voice down, boy. We don't want the neighbours waking up. Get a hold of yourself.'

Errol collapsed on a chair near the door, wrapping his arms round his body, his teeth beginning to chatter.

'What we've got to do,' said Mr Didcot, 'is to put on our thinking caps.' Errol's collapse seemed to have calmed him. He regarded the ungainly object on the divan thoughtfully, pursing his lips. 'What we have here, son, is a problem of logistics. X has to be moved from A to B and the problem is how. I can't manage her myself.'

'You mean you've touched her?'

'Of course I've touched her. You don't think I'd have woke you up this time if I could've managed on my own? We've got to get her downstairs.'

'I won't.'

'We've got to get her downstairs and out to the Anderson. Then it's plain sailing.'

'I won't do it!'

'I've told you before, Errol, keep your voice down.'

'I'll call the cops.' He stood up wildly.

'You'll do no such thing. You don't think I want Mother bothered with a lot of policemen?'

'But you can't just . . .' He sat down again, staring.

'Oh yes I can, son. It's worked before.'

'Before? You mean you've done this before?'

Colour came up in Mr Didcot's face and he looked put out. He sat down on the chair by the desk, rearranging the pencils and piles of manuscripts there. 'It was an accident,' he said brusquely.

'And what was this?' He nodded, but could not look, towards the divan.

'This was different. I never laid a finger on this one.'

'How'd she get here then? How'd you get her here? She didn't walk up here by herself.'

'Yes she did. They'll go with anyone, that kind. Offer them anything – drinks, a bed, drugs, sex – they'll follow anyone. Like lady dogs. Trouble is, you don't know where they've bin first.'

There was silence for a moment, broken only by the

hiss of the gas fire, Mr Didcot looking thoughtfully at the divan, Errol helplessly at him. Judicially Mr Didcot continued, 'She must've bin drinking before I found her. That's what it must've bin. Or drugs, perhaps. Up to anything they are these days. If she'd bin drinking or anything else, you don't know what effect the pills'll have. You simply can't tell.'

'You give her pills?'

'Only Mother's sleeping pills, nothing injurious. Offer them anything, they'll take them. By the time they get up here they're out on their feet. Don't know nothing. Nice and quiet, no harm done. Only trouble is, you don't know where they've bin first. They could be full of something really injurious. That must be the explanation.' He paused. 'It's their own fault really. I mean, you'd think they'd know what they was doing. This one, for instance – all that fat on her. Unhealthy. You'd think she'd have more sense than to fill herself up with pills off a stranger when she's bin drinking. I mean, it's a strain on the heart when you're carrying the weight she is. Stands to reason. The other one, that was different. Not the one you saw – like I said, she come to in due course and walked out of here right as rain, hadn't a clue. That's the usual way, no harm done. But the other one, a year or two back, that was an accident. The pills didn't hardly seem to have no effect on that one, just put her out for half an hour or so and then she come to again in the middle, yelling blue murder. She didn't ought to've done that. These old houses aren't soundproof.'

He straightened up, speaking more briskly. 'Still,

there wasn't much of a problem with that one. She was only a little bit of a thing. I could manage her by myself easy. Anyway, it was long before you come, a thing of the past. This one's more of a problem, twelve stone if she's a pound.'

Errol whispered, 'I won't.'

'What's the alternative? You tell me that. We could call the police and explain what happened but we don't want them poking about in the Anderson, do we, asking a lot of questions, upsetting Mother. She's never bin strong, not since her operation. Years ago that was, soon after my boy passed on. A lady's operation it was, if you understand me. Put an end to our married life. There's people say now it makes no difference, but I couldn't fancy relations with her after that. Unnatural, somehow. She's easily upset; you saw that when you talked of leaving. We don't want to upset her again.'

'I'm not staying here now.'

'We don't want no more of that.' He rose and suddenly, in the small hot room in the dead middle of the night, he seemed to tower, his head to reach the shadowed ceiling, his arms long to sinewy hands, his eyes a fiery steel. 'You're staying and that's final. I want you here. You add something, something bizarre. I like it better with you here. You're staying.'

Hardly heard, he whispered again, 'I won't.'

'Oh yes you will, son. Because I'm in charge, see, I'm the master. My brain is a thousand times better fitted to work things out than yours is, whatever they say. D'you honestly think that the brain that worked out all this . . .' he gestured towards the desk, 'and which is at work on an even more intricate and astounding revelation which one day soon I may reveal to you, is going to be defied by someone like you? No, son . . .' His voice grew kindly and he moved forward to lay his hand caressingly on Errol's shoulder, running his fingers up the strong black muscles of his neck to ruffle the close hair. 'You're staying with me, son, so don't let's have any more nonsense about that.' His hand lingered, stroked, smoothed, a smile on his pale lips, his eyes dreamy. Beneath his hand Errol froze like a cat. The thumping of his heart seemed louder than the hiss of the gas fire.

Mr Didcot recovered himself and moved away. 'Well, we'd better get on with it. We get her downstairs to the toilet and then I'll unlock the Anderson.'

'No.' But it was faint.

'Come on now. You take her shoulders, I'll take her feet. Open the door first. Get moving.'

As though in a trance Errol got slowly to his feet and opened the door. Mr Didcot had gathered the fat legs together and gave them a tug. The body wobbled and shifted a little, the head flopping sideways.

'Turn the landing light on. We need to see what we're doing.' Errol did so. 'Now then, get a good grip on her shoulders and we're away.'

Shuffling, puffing, but surprisingly silently, they got her down the stairs, past Nelly's shut door, along the short passage. Mr Didcot put down his end and unlocked the back door, then hefted her up again to dump her just inside the the lavatory. He took out a handkerchief, white in the darkness, and wiped his forehead, while Errol leaned back against the lintel and shut his eyes, his legs scarcely holding him up. The air smelled moistly sweet against the acrid smell of the lavatory. The orange glow of London was reflected on the quilted underside of the clouds. There was absolute silence.

'You wait here. I won't be a jiffy.'

Feeling about inside the lavatory walls, Mr Didcot unhooked a key and went down the path into the darkness towards the hump of the Anderson shelter. Ducking down the muddy steps, he looked sharply left and right behind him, but there were no lighted windows anywhere, only darkness and silence and a soft rain. He turned the key without much difficulty but the door stuck a little and he had to give it a push. When the shelter had been built he had laid boards and then linoleum over the floor, so the place was comparatively dry. He had never let it crumble into decay nor tried to demolish it for, as a student of history, he was pessimistic over the probability of never needing it again. As it happened, of course, he had been right.

The smell that came from the opened door was peculiar.

He went back to where Errol languished against the wall. 'Right,' he whispered, 'just give me a hand as far as the steps and then I'll fend for myself. Quietly, now.'

They heaved up the dead weight once more and staggered with it down to the black mouth of the shelter. Dumping her at the foot of the steps, Errol's knees did give way and he collapsed on the top one, his head and hands hanging.

Mr Didcot gave him a sharp look. 'You get back to the house. I can manage. And put the kettle on. We could both do with a cup of tea. Go on, now.'

He watched while Errol got to his feet and staggered back to the house; saw the light come on in the kitchen and Errol weave across to the sink. The light reached out almost to the shelter steps, and Mr Didcot quickly set about hauling the body inside.

When he entered the kitchen Errol was sitting with his head in his hands. His skin looked lilac-coloured. There was a smell of vomit and Mr Didcot went to the sink and turned the tap full on, washed his hands, then made the tea, for the kettle was boiling. He spooned sugar into both cups and pushed one towards Errol. 'Here, drink that.' He sat down the other side of the table and stirred his tea; the spoon rattled, for now his hands were trembling. He took out his handkerchief and wiped his face again, his eyes set in deep hollows by the overhead light.

From behind his hands Errol said, 'You'll be caught.'

Mr Didcot smiled. 'Who by?'

'The fuzz. Her people . . .'

'A girl like that hasn't got no people. There's hundreds of girls go missing every week and who bothers about them? Who d'you think'd bother about you if you was to go missing one day – except for me and Mother, of course, now.'

Errol raised his head and stared across at him. 'I won't help you.'

Mr Didcot said gently, 'You already have, son. If anything was to come out now you'd find yourself in Queer Street. You know what the coppers are like.'

There was a very long silence, during which all the light seemed to be drawn from Errol's face by Mr Didcot's benign but unwavering stare.

When Errol's head drooped again Mr Didcot finished his tea. 'The situation's not ideal,' he said. 'I had considered that plastic bag the Council give out when the dustmen was on strike and we never got round to using – but on balance I decided against it. She's better where she is, at least for the moment. After all, no one never come after that other one. So long as no one misses them, who's to know they're gone?'

Errol began to cry. The tears ran down the lilac skin of his face and dripped on to his pyjamas. Mr Didcot got to his feet and rinsed out the cups in the sink.

'You cut along back to bed. You'll feel better in the morning.'

SEVEN

Mr Didcot walks briskly, avoiding the puddles, his lips pursing at the detritus of yesterday's Bank Holiday awash in the gutters, the rain sluicing off the big umbrella, wetting the skirts of his raincoat. The streets have a sluggish air, for what with the weather and the holiday, a certain number of bus crews have not turned up for duty and the service is infrequent. The newsagent at the corner has not hung out his rack of newspapers, and his cat is sitting morosely on a pile of *London Advertisers* on the counter instead of on the doorstep as is his custom.

There is more life in the High Street – heavy traffic sizzling past in muddy waves, the lights on in the shops, and plastic-hooded housewives stocking up on things they have run out of over the long Easter weekend. Mr Didcot has not run out of anything; he is a provident shopper, and all he needs today is a loaf of bread which he can buy at Mansfield's – into whose door he turns, closing and shaking his umbrella before entering. The shop is almost empty, which is just as well as only one assistant has turned up and she is serving. Mr Didcot loiters by the deep freeze, then makes his way to the back of the shop, from which the manager defensively appears.

'Can I help you?'

'Ah – Mr Abbott. You won't remember me.'

'Oh yes?' He surveys the neatly smiling man suspiciously while memory stirs. 'Oh yes, it's Mr . . .'

'Mr Didcot, that's right. Your young chap Errol lodges with me and my good lady.'

'Ah.' The manager looks sour. 'He's not turned up again this morning. Look at it – only one assistant and all the books to do!'

'It's not what you think. No Bank Holiday hang-over for our Errol – he's a good steady lad. At least –' a thought flits behind his eyes, 'at least so me and Mrs Didcot's always found, although you can't really tell, can you, you can only speak as you find. Anyway, he's not swinging the lead this morning, he's queer again.'

'What is it, flu?'

'No. It's more like his nerves.'

'Nerves?'

'Yes. High-strung those chaps are, you know, not like you and me. Don't know what goes on in their heads half the time. But he's got a bit of a cough again, he must've caught cold somewhere.'

'Well – I'll need a certificate if he's more than the three days.'

Mr Didcot laughed. 'Oh he'll be back before then, don't you worry, Mr Abbott. It's only his nerves really. I said I'd pop round and tell you.'

'That's very kind of you.'

'Not at all. It's no trouble. Satisfactory, is he?'

'Very. Very quiet, not like some of his kind.'

'Yes, he's a quiet lad. Bit simple, perhaps?'

'He's a good worker.'

'Friendly, is he?'

The manager bridled. 'There's only me and the young ladies. He'd hardly . . .'

'No, no, of course not.' Mr Didcot looks round the shop. 'Now I wonder if I might trouble you for a small sliced loaf?'

Smiling, polite, he takes his purchase, says Good-day and goes outside, pausing to open the umbrella, then turns down the High Street towards the Public Library, for great new concepts to do with the Prince Regent's daughter have been swelling in his mind over the last few weeks. On the way he stops on impulse and buys an early *Evening Standard*. There is hardly anything in it but Sport and City; he hasn't really expected anything else, but it never hurts to make sure. He takes a look at the horoscope. 'You will be on top of the world,' he reads. 'A great day for getting things done, making decisions for yourself and younger friends. Go ahead with confidence.'

He closes the paper, folds it neatly, puts it in his raincoat pocket. 'Poppycock,' he says, but he is smiling.

He goes on, and up the steps of the Library for a good morning of research.

Errol lay motionless on the camp bed, his eyes shut, in a sort of sleep. When awakening came too near he willed himself back into a nullity, a suspension of contact with thought or action, a deliberate catalepsy. Sometimes he coughed. He was cold yet sweated. His skin had lost all gloss and fullness, as though vitality had dwindled to the tiny buried seed that kept his heart beating. He had drunk the tea that Mr Didcot had brought up to him but had not touched the bread and margarine. Time, weather, duties did not exist for him; he simply was because as yet there had not been time for him to cease to be. His ancestors would have known how to do it.

He lay; and the rain poured down and later slackened and by tea time stopped. The room grew lighter as the sun came out before setting, and then sank into twilight again. Behind his closed eyes he sensed all this but did not care. He had moved only to use the chamber under the bed. He had not drunk the second cup of tea Mr Didcot brought him; he had heard but not taken in his rallying words. A smell of frying came up at supper time but he did not respond. Night came.

Nelly came.

It took her twenty-five minutes, hauling herself from stair to stair by banisters that creaked at her grasp, resting and gasping halfway up, sitting for a while on the top stair of the landing outside Mr Didcot's two closed doors, feeling the great leaps of her heart behind the cascades of flesh and the pain running up and down the rigid veins of her legs. Then on again up the second flight to the attic, wheezing like an old dog, grasping the door handle of the room and leaning there, trembling, as it swung open under her weight and half-pulled her into the room, which was dark and humped with thick shapes of furniture and junk mysterious in the glow from the street lamps.

'Errol?' Her voice quavered. 'You there, Errol?'

There was no sound, but in the darkness his eyes opened.

'Errol? It's me, dear. Are you all right?'

'Ma.'

'I got to sit down. Oh my!'

'Ma?'

'Have you got a chair, dear? I got to sit down.'

There was a rustle of bed clothes thrown back, his white-pyjama'd body and white eyes moved towards her in the darkness, his dark hands took her weight.

'Ma? How d'you get up here?'

'Don't ask me, dear. It's surprising what you can do if you try.'

'Here . . .' He supported her a few steps and knocked aside his yesterday's clothing from a wooden chair. She sagged onto it, pressing her hand to her breasts, gasping and laughing. He squatted beside her, holding her other hand tightly and staring up into her face. 'You okay?'

'I'll be all right in a minute. Put your coat on, dear, you'll catch cold.'

He got up and put his jacket round his shoulders. 'You've never come up them stairs, never.'

'That's right, dear. Not since – oh, ever such a long time. Ten, twelve years it must be. My word! You'll have to carry me down!'

He hunched on the edge of the bed, staring at her wildly. 'You shouldn't come up here!'

'I was worried about you. I couldn't get no sense out of Dad.'

'He knows you're here?'

'No, dear, no. He'd never believe it, would he, not in a month of Sundays. No, he's gone to his work as usual and I was sitting there worrying and listening and knowing you'd not had a bite to eat and thinking about your chest, and I said to myself I said Nelly, get up them stairs!' She chuckled. 'That's a kind of a saucy catchphrase, dear, you wouldn't know it. Get up them stairs, I said – and here I am.'

'You mustn't come here! You mustn't let him know you come up here.'

'Whyever not, dear? I was worried about you. Are you coughing? You never had no hot water-bottle nor nothing, and nothing to eat.'

'You mustn't tell him! He mustn't know you can get upstairs . . .'

'I don't expect he'd believe it, not unless he saw it with his own eyes. I suppose I might've bin able to get about more after all, these last years, only I never had the reason to try. We got real set in our ways, me and Dad, till you come to shake us up a bit. How you feeling, dear? You ought to get back into bed.'

'I'm okay. I got to get you downstairs.' He stood up abruptly and started coughing.

'There now! You've got that nasty cough back. I said to Dad Is he coughing? and he said Not so's you'd notice it and I said to myself Well, what does that mean, is he or isn't he? and you are. You get back into bed.'

'No.' He began pulling his jeans on over his pyjamas, and then a sweater. 'I got to get you downstairs.'

She sat square and obstinate. 'You let that cough get a hold on you again and I'll make Dad fetch the doctor to you. He used to call regular when my legs was first bad but now they're chronic he doesn't. Run off their feet, doctors are, and Dad can easy fetch my pills and the prescription when it runs out, it's no trouble, he's done it for years, no need to trouble the doctor. But you play fast and loose with that chest of yours, my lad, and I'll have him after you!'

'I'm all right, Ma.'

'Yes. It sounds like it!'

'Ma.' He bent and took her thick hands in his tensely. 'Ma, you got to promise. We don't want no doctor, we don't want no one here. You got to promise.'

'There's nothing wrong in seeing the doctor . . .'

'I won't have him, d'you hear? He mustn't come here! I hate doctors, I won't have no one messing about . . .'

'All right, dear, all right. Only I'm not having you down with that chest again.'

'You got to promise . . .'

'All right, dear, I promise.'

'And you mustn't let no one know you come up those stairs.'

'What, not even Dad?'

'No one, no one! No one's to know you can move about.'

'Well, I can't hardly. I don't know how I done it, I don't really. I was worried, see, and I said Nelly, I said, get up them stairs. He'd never believe it!'

'He mustn't! He mustn't never have no idea. You

got to promise.' He shook both her hands between his, trying to shake some sense into her.

She smiled at him fondly in the darkness, in which both of them now could see quite well. 'You are a funny boy and no mistake. All this carry-on because I managed to stir my poor old stumps. You ought to be pleased.'

'Okay, I'm pleased. It's great, I'm pleased. But you don't tell no one – not no one.'

'All right, you soppy thing. I won't tell no one. It's our secret, eh?'

'You promise? Solemn?'

'Scout's honour, dear. Was you ever a Scout?'

'No.'

'My Terry was. He used to go camping. Stung by a wasp he was once. Blue bags – no one has blue bags now.'

'I got to get you downstairs.'

'Haven't you made it cosy up here! All your clothes hanging up. And your pictures. I expect Dad's told you to use whatever you like up here to make yourself comfortable. There's a lot of Terry's stuff – his little cot – and there's his stamp albums somewhere and his Meccano. Dad wouldn't get rid of it. Kept that back room just as it was for years – that was Terry's room, see. He used to go and sit in it, hour after hour, Dad did, when Terry was taken. And then gradual he got started on his Project and turned it into the Den. I never bin in it since he turned it into the Den.'

'Come on, Ma.'

Reluctantly she allowed him to heave her to her feet.

They shuffled out onto the landing and there her legs gave way and, with him descending anxiously before her, she sat her way down from stair to stair, pulling her skirt modestly down over her creased knees, hauled to her feet again to pass by Mr Didcot's doors, to sit the rest of the way and reach at last the kitchen.

Puffing, her heart thumping again, but with colour in her cheeks and eyes bright, she eased herself round the table. 'You sit down, dear, get near the fire. You don't want to take cold now, after being in bed all day. I'll make you some supper. You've had nothing to eat since yesterday. Shall I scramble an egg? That's light. Could you fancy a scrambled egg?'

It was her bed time when he had eaten. He washed the crockery while she made both of them hot water-bottles. He helped her into her room, sat her on the edge of the bed, knelt and removed the slippers from her bulging feet. She stroked his close hair.

'You go straight to bed, now.'

'Okay.'

'And watch that cough.'

'I'm not coughing.'

'Nor you are. You take care, though.'

He stood up. 'And you promised, okay?'

'Our secret.'

'And you don't try it again, eh?'

'You're a bully, that's what you are.'

'I mean it, Ma. Please.'

'Very well, dear. You're a good boy.'

He bent and kissed her cheek. 'I got to keep you safe.'

He went back to work next day. Mr Abbott was pleasantly surprised to see him.

Thereafter Errol stayed closer to home than ever. He gave up going to the café, for everyone talked and laughed there, you could not but help being drawn in, even a little. When he did not, they cooled; they looked at him with marble eyes and began jeering at his lack of black identity. He had always held aloof; now he closed himself completely. He made them itch.

He stopped going there. If he wanted a coke or a glass of milk there was a coffee stall, where sometimes a half-drunk Irishman muttered offensively, or the multiple tea shops, where no one cared; or he bought milk from a milk machine and drank it where he stood.

As the days lengthened he still went walking sometimes after supper but not for so long. Walking fast, shoulders hunched, he would return quickly, enter the kitchen to make sure Nelly was still there, snug in her chair or pottering at the sink. 'How you bin? You not bin upstairs again?' he would ask urgently, and she would chuckle and pat his tense arm and say, 'Whatever would I be doing that for? Silly chump!'

Once he found her with a dustpan and brush, sitting on the bottom stair in the hall. 'I'll do that,' he said and took the implements away from her.

'It's nice to move about a bit.'

'Don't you never try them stairs again, Ma. You promised me.'

'You are a funny boy.'

He did not smile. 'I'm not joking.'

'No need to get huffy.' She hauled herself to her feet by the banisters. 'I'd've thought you'd be glad I was trying to get about a bit more.'

'It's not safe.'

'Get away with you!'

'It's not safe,' he repeated sombrely. 'I don't want you moving about without I'm here.'

She humoured him and did not try the stairs. But sometimes during the day when he was at work and Mr Didcot shut away in the Den, she would take a little walk round and round the kitchen table, trying to avoid supporting herself too much on the furniture, or shuffle up and down the narrow hall, from front door to back door, steadying herself against the wall. Her legs throbbed and trembled and she got out of breath; but little by little it became easier. She was pleased. Perhaps one day she could get out of doors. She would surprise everyone in time.

Errol avoided Mr Didcot as much as possible, evading the Sunday walks by going out on his own or upstairs to sleep before Mr Didcot was ready. Mr Didcot seemed unconcerned; his views on current affairs did not diminish and he was certain that his plans for dealing with inflation, strikes and other urban ills would solve the Government's problems; but sometimes, at Errol's silence and his eyes that obstinately never now looked at Mr Didcot, a glint of some emotion passed behind his prim face and bland expression – anger, perhaps, but also pain. And puzzlement.

On early closing day Errol always went direct from work to the public wash-house, putting his laundry into the washing-machines and himself into one of the cubicled baths, where he ate a cheese roll and drank a carton of milk. One afternoon in late May he found Mr Didcot waiting outside for him.

There was nothing he could do, after his first instinctive thoughts of flight, but walk along with him, for Mr Didcot knew very well that he would be taking the laundry straight home. Going along the High Street he was offered a cup of tea but refused. Mr Didcot looked at him pensively, having to walk rather faster than his usual pace to keep up with Errol's haste. Turning the corner into Wardlow Road he puffed, 'Hold hard, son, where's the fire?' As they slowed down a little, he took off his cap and fanned himself humorously with it. 'You young chaps! Full of vim and vigour, you are, not like us poor old grand-pas. Listen, son, I want a word with you.'

'No.'

'What d'you mean, no? You're a funny one and no mistake. I want a word with you private but some-how or other I have the feeling you've bin avoiding me. I broke into an afternoon's research to run you to earth today – and it's at a crucial point too, crucial. I'm on the very verge of new horizons. The least you can do is give me five minutes of your valuable time.'

Errol halted, looking down at the polythene bag of laundry in his hands. 'What d'you want?'

'Come with me. We can't talk here.'

He moved on, turning down a side street at the end

of which lay a little square of grass, remnant of some ancient village green, now set with two iron seats and a man's urinal. Under a chestnut tree, beaten into sterility by the missiles of conker-mad urchins every autumn, the grass was strewn with crusts and pigeons. Two old men were on one seat but the other was free. Apart from the croaking of the old men and the constant shifting of the pigeons, the place was quiet, children at school, houses uninhabited, no through traffic.

'You ought to've seen this place during the dustmen's strike,' said Mr Didcot, sitting down. 'Piled high with garbage, it was, sacks and cartons, paper bags and just plain rotten rubbish. You never seen such a disgusting sight. Playing fast and loose with the nation's health and not a word from the Government. No direction, no authority. I tell you, one lot's as bad as the other. It's a wonder we wasn't all struck down with some epidemic, the way they let the stuff pile up. What this nation needs is firm government. And we don't get it, we don't get it.' He shook his head and was silent for a moment, then drew his attention back to Errol, who had sat down the other end of the seat, his laundry on the ground by his feet. He sat with bent head and downcast eyes, as withdrawn as though a cloak were over him.

Mr Didcot moved nearer, laid a hand on his arm and said softly, 'Son, are you avoiding me?'

Errol snatched his arm away, jerking his head up and staring at him wildly.

'I don't want you should be avoiding me. If I spoke

to you sharp the other night it was just because I was upset. I didn't like you talking about leaving again.' He put his hand out once more and laid it on Errol's knee. It quivered, boney and smooth under the denim. 'I miss our talks, Errol. It's lonely work, intellectual researches like I'm engaged in. I couldn't expect you to follow me in the half of it but you give me something back, son, just being there, listening. These last weeks it's not bin the same . . .' His fingers caressed the cloth. 'I've had, as it were, no sounding-board. And I'm on to something big, son, something really big. It's the breakthrough to a new development in my concept of history, beyond even my first original theories. Mind you, it upsets some of the ones I've bin acting on over the years but I'm big enough to admit mistakes. All great thinkers are big enough to admit mistakes. I want to tell you about it. You don't very likely follow it all but I want to tell you. We could go home and I'd show you my new graphs.'

'No!' He jerked away.

Mr Didcot withdrew his hand and folded them together in his lap, looking down at them with eyes suddenly hazed. His voice was low. 'Whatever has bin in the past, Errol, has nothing to do with you and me. It was an – an irrevelance. I called on you in an emergency because I feel close to you. You've brought something into my life that I've bin lonely for all these years.'

'Yeah?' His lips snarled back. 'What about – them?'

'It's hard for you to understand – you with all your

youth and vigour. You could get anyone you liked, you could, with them long legs and the shoulders on you and all they always say about black men. You could have anyone you liked if you wasn't shy – you're too shy, son. You got no reason to be shy. Now I got reason. I was brought up shy. I saw my mother in her birthday suit once when I was a little lad and my dad beat the daylights out of me. Thrashed me within an inch of my life, he did – and her too. With his belt. He taught me what was decent. I've never seen a naked woman since, not in the flesh. I made sure me and Mrs Didcot was always decent – and then there was her operation. Couldn't go on after that. You wouldn't understand. You with your looks and your age, you could have anyone . . . I often picture you with some girl, larking about, hugging and kissing and that – having kiddies, perhaps, laughing and innocent, you know, like Adam and Eve. Adam, see, A – it all comes back to it.'

There was silence, Errol hunched sullenly, Mr Didcot looking down at his clasped hands. Behind them the pigeons rustled among the crusts.

'You mean a lot to me, Errol, I don't mind admitting it. It's funny really – I mean, seeing the difference there is between you and me. I don't want nothing to come between us.'

'What about – them?' Errol repeated.

'That was unfortunate. But it's all in the past. There's no need ever to think of it again.'

'But – they're there!'

'But no one knows it save you and me.' He looked

at him slyly. 'And we're safe enough, aren't we? Neither you nor me's likely to go gossipping, are we?'

Errol's head drooped. He ran one long hand over his face as though trying to wipe away a cobweb.

Mr Didcot watched him tenderly. 'You put the past out of your mind, Errol. Put yourself in my hands, I know what's best. With me to guide you, I can enlarge your horizons far beyond what anyone'd think possible. I don't believe what people say about only just coming down off the trees. Under my guidance there's no reason why in time you shouldn't be able to follow at least half of my thinking. It's important to both of us. Trust me, son.'

Errol said nothing but still sat drooping, the bag of laundry between his feet. Mr Didcot smiled, studying the close black head, the delicate ears, the smooth tendons of neck and shoulders inside the jacket, the flat pale-lined hands, the tight thighs. He sighed, reached out and pressed the boy's shoulder, then stood up, settling his raincoat and the cap on his neat head.

'Will you come along, then? I've interfered with my afternoon's study to have this chat, you know.'

'I'll stay here.'

'Very well.' He buttoned his raincoat. 'You'll be back for your tea, though.' Errol still did not lift his head. 'Don't be late, now.' Hesitantly he moved away; then, straightening his shoulders, he gained his usual brisk pace and moved out of sight.

Errol walks. The seat grew hard, the wind freshened, the two old men had gone.

He hefts the laundry bag and walks at random, far away from Wardlow Road, from the High Street, from Scholars Town, through side roads where he has never been before. Locked Baptist chapels; terraces of grey brick or flaking stucco, old dogs sleep on their pavements; and soon school children shout and run, bang gates and knockers, push each other off the kerb, trail at the handles of their siblings' prams with mothers who want cups of tea. There are warehouses and small engineering works; a sudden canal, sluggish and edged with black machinery; small shops with grubby windows; Labour committee rooms; a pub, shut; thin terraced houses rotting behind frail Victorian balconies; an all-night garage, a depot for British Road lorries, a fish-and-chip shop, closed; pigeons, black walls and soot, archways and heavy traffic; bus stops, taxi ranks, one-way streets; a railway terminus.

Standing beside the unwiped counter of a snack bar, he drinks a cup of tea. No one looks at him, not even when he gives his order, pays. No one looks at anyone, or speaks, munching their pies and doughnuts, swilling their liquids against the pulsing traffic outside. It is nearly rush hour and queues are beginning to form at the bus stops, to push through the arches of the terminus.

Errol joins them. He wanders from platform to platform, reading the places that the trains will go to, buffeted by people catching them and impatient of his drifting. Huge voices echo information from the roof, doors slam, luggage trailers hiss to and fro, and always there is the flurry of movement, voices, feet, among which the ubiquitous pigeons bustle.

He stands, staring down an empty platform from behind the closed gate, his bag of laundry hanging at his side. A train has just gone out and there is nothing there now save empty trolleys. A porter far blacker than himself slots in a new place-name and already a queue is forming, restive, evening newspapers under their arms, jostling Errol to be in the queue or to get out of it. Above the sooty cavern there is space and sky, beyond the empty rails there is space and new places, freedom, escape. Anonymity, loneliness.

He rubs his hand over his face, closing his eyes for a moment, then turns to push his way against the incoming crowds, out into the forecourt, the traffic, the lights, to cross the main road and turn north again, back towards Wardlow Road. He takes a different way, the direct way this time as well as he can judge, down larger streets, with pubs and chain stores, and a police station. His pace checks here and he looks in through the open doors. A policeman is standing there and glances at the bundle hanging from Errol's hand; it is a plastic bag and he can see that it contains nothing but laundry. His glance flicks up and Errol's flicks away, and his feet hurry him on, long strides, not running but fast away from the policeman and the blue lamp and the advertisements for burglars and missing persons and the cells behind.

He is late home for supper, but Nelly has kept it hot for him.

Mr Didcot, getting ready to go out, looks at him coolly. 'Bin for a walk, have you?'

'That's nice, dear,' Nelly says. 'Where did you go?'
'Nowhere,' Errol says.

So although Mr Didcot could not persuade Errol inside the Den ever again, their Sunday walks resumed and the long monologues, punctuated less than ever by any comment from Errol. Mr Didcot appeared oblivious to how silent he had become, spinning the cocoon of his own words with even greater zest now that there was no interruption, a cocoon which held the two men tightly together, passive and active, possessed and possessor.

His newest researches concerned Princess Charlotte's Christian names – for who could dispute that had she not died in childbirth the whole course of British history would have been different? This line of thinking had opened up a whole new field of study, for whereas he had long grasped the significance of the fact that the names of English monarchs were not necessarily those by which they were called within the family (there were Alberts, Augustuses, Alfreds who had ascended the throne as George or Edward) he had only recently had his eyes opened to the female line, where the mystic letter A abounded, even if often in second place. The theory, said Mr Didcot, pacing briskly over the tarmac paths of Parliament Hill, his pale eyes fixed on history, stood up more and more firmly the deeper it was explored. It revolutionised not only his own but Great Britain's historical destiny. One must look far into the future as well as the past – for even a simpleton could not ignore the fact that now we have a

Princess Anne.

His theories so absorbed him that he paid no attention to the girls they saw around them, in the streets or spread about on the grass. He had Errol and he had his researches; for the time being he needed nothing else, although he still left the house after supper each evening and came back after the others were asleep. Sometimes he still crept up the stairs to the attic and stood in the darkness listening to Errol's breath, but he never now went inside. He was satisfied.

So the weeks passed and it was June – a fine June, Wimbledon weather, raining only for Ascot. The streets smelled of hot dust and privet, diesel fumes and the drenching sweetness of syringa, and old trees of lilac and laburnum astonished with their sheeting colours that lasted longer than usual above the walls and dustbins at their roots. Old women revealed their upper arms in sleeveless dresses and labourers stripped sweatily to their tanned waists. Nelly dragged a chair to the open back door and sat there often; unless the wind was blowing from the east, the lavatory smell was hardly noticeable. All sorts of weeds and residual flowers had blossomed in the garden and the hump of the Anderson shelter was pretty with dandelions and chickweed, and clumps of camomile at its base. The ramblers would soon be out, and the big old lupins. The rank grass was scattered with a dozen different weeds, flat little plantains, daisies, a small mauve flower that seeded anywhere, and along the fence convolvulus had begun its steely advance. Sometimes pairs of white butterflies flicked past and blackbirds sang.

She sat, spilling over the hard chair, gazing and dozing, remembering phrases from her girlhood about lovesome spots and being nearer God's heart in a garden – certainly nearer than in one of them tower blocks, even if they were high, she thought, and had a little laugh to herself. When the ramblers were out perhaps she'd manage to pick some. The warm weather suited her legs, and she could walk a little way now without holding on to anything at all, if she took it slowly.

When the air letter came, she was alone. It came by the second post and Mr Didcot was out at the shops. She heard the unaccustomed flap of the letterbox and shuffled out to see what it could be, and there was the letter, lying on the linoleum. She shuffled along and wheezily picked it up, carrying it back to the kitchen with some excitement. She had never seen an air letter before and turned it this way and that before finding her spectacles and reading Errol's name and on the other side that of the sender, Mrs Lucille Baker, from an address in Kingston, Jamaica.

'Well I never!' She stared at it, her heart thumping and her face feeling hot. 'Well I never! However did this get here? Goodness!' She stood, her thoughts in a flurry, the flimsy flat paper as potent as a bomb. How? And what? Loving or upsetting? From Jamaica – palm trees, sun and laughing black faces, rich Americans and people like Sir Noel Coward. All that way, across the sea, through the sky, from unknown black hands to her, standing in the kitchen with it between her own knobbly fingers. How did one open it? What did it say? Was it good or bad for her Errol?

When she heard the front door open she instinctively, without thought, thrust the letter deep into the pocket of her overall so that her husband should not know of its existence, and she made her face empty, her movements calm as ever, so that he should not guess the excitement in her mind.

That evening, when they were alone after Mr Didcot's customary departure, she drew it out again and put it into Errol's hand. He stared at it almost as she had done and his face seemed to glow, as though the blood had rush up under the skin.

'It come this morning,' she said.

'It's from my auntie.'

'I guessed it was. Did you write, then?'

'Yes.'

'And never told me? You are a funny boy. After me going on at you so long to write and all.' She peered at him reproachfully, making her way round the table to her chair. 'When did you write, then?'

'A few weeks back. After Bank Holiday.'

'Well, I'm glad you did, dear. She must've bin worrying.' She sank down among the cushions. 'Go on, open it.'

He turned it over and read the address on the back, then cautiously began to open it. It tore raggedly, and with some awe they both watched its ingenious unfolding. He began to read, and her gaze went from the paper to his face as, absorbed, his lips moving a little, he slowly took in the words. When he had done, he looked up, his face glowing.

'They're great. They're all great. Emmeline's going

to get married.'

'That's nice.'

'The boys are great. After school they run wild, she says. They've got a dog.'

'Fancy!'

He looked at the letter again. 'My uncle's with the Post Office. They've got a house on the edge of town. And auntie runs the Church ladies.' He laughed, a wide, joyous laugh with no reservations. 'That's my auntie all right! She'll run anything! Emmeline's boy's on the *Gleaner* – that's the big paper there, she says. She got a job, typing there, and met him. She says Emmeline's done okay for herself, going up in the world. She's getting married in September.'

'Well I never!'

'She says they'll send me the fare.'

A great wave of coldness enveloped her. 'The fare?'

'For the wedding. They want me there. She says I can live with them.'

'Leave England?'

'She says things aren't too good there, but they bin lucky. She says I can live with them.' He began to move about the room, his long limbs restless with joy, his face shining. 'I'll find work. My auntie'll fix it. Or Emmeline. She'll get her boy to find me something. She's like my auntie, a ball of fire once she's started. She says its warm all the time, people go in the sea all the time. Here, you read it.' He thrust the letter at her.

She shook her head. 'I haven't got my glasses.'

'Here . . .' He took them from the mantlepiece.

'No, I don't want to read it. It's enough you telling me.' She bent her head over the hands clasped tightly in her lap.

He stared at her rough grey hair and the joy went out of him. He squatted down in front of her. 'Ma?'

'You'll like it there, dear. I can just see you, in and out of the waves in the sunshine, all wet and shining.'

'Ma.'

She looked up, smiling as well as she could. A tear wandered slowly down the grooves and hollows of her face and she wiped it off. 'I'm all right, dear. It's just the shock.'

'I want to go, Ma.'

'I know you do, dear.'

'This place is no good for me.'

'You've bin moody lately. I can tell.'

'You bin good to me.'

'You've bin good to me too, dear, me and Dad. You brought a little sunshine into our lives.' She put out a hand and he took it. 'Well, all good things come to an end.'

'Don't tell him.'

They stared at each other, he urgent, she perplexed.

'He's got to know sometime.'

'Not yet. Don't tell him yet.'

She pondered. 'It'll upset him.'

'You hid the letter.'

'Yes.' She pondered more. 'He's funny sometimes. I didn't know how he'd take it, not till I knew what it was. He's a mystery sometimes.'

'I want to go.'

'Yes, you must go. Now you got the chance. It's not much of a life for you here, just with me and Dad. And Dad with his ideas – he's a bit overwhelming sometimes, the way he goes on, I can't follow it all. It's as though he was eating one up.'

'Not you, Ma. I don't want to leave you.'

She squeezed his hand. 'You're a good boy, Errol.'

'Don't tell him, eh? Not till I got the ticket.'

'And then you'll tell him yourself? You got to stand on your own feet.'

'Okay.'

'You don't need to be afraid of him, you know. He's funny sometimes but he thinks the world of you. I just don't know what he'll do when you're gone.'

Through the kitchen window the tangled garden was a square of gold in the evening sunlight, the kitchen filling up with dusk. He shivered. She squeezed his hand again, giving it a little shake. 'And think what that lovely sunshine'll do for your chest. No more coughs. You won't know yourself.'

'Maybe when I'm rich I'll send for you, eh?'

'My island of dreams? Remember that song that Harry Belafonte did?' She began to sing, her voice cracked but sweet. 'Oh island in the sun . . .'

He took it up, exaggerating the West Indian accent, '. . . Given to me by my father's hand . . .' They finished the song together, Nelly laughing and wiping her eyes, Errol full of joy again. He stood upright. 'I'll have to learn to talk the island way. No dirty cockney no more. No Enoch Powell no more. I'll write her tomorrow, tell her to send that ticket.'

He stood, tall and taut, seeming to shine in the darkening kitchen, a boy suddenly freed in his own skin, a spring ready to leap.

So next day he went in his lunch hour to buy an air letter and wrote to his aunt, standing at one of the Post Office shelves, with its crumbling blotting-paper, chained pens and telegram forms, writing slowly, tense with concentration and hope; posted it; and waited. But waited with his head up, his movements resilient, bought himself a pink shirt and a pair of striped jeans, strolled round Woolworths and the Co-op considering what presents he could take, looked at posters in travel agents' windows.

'Errol's a bit more cheerful these days,' said Mr Didcot over his midday steakburger and mashed potatoes, 'I wonder what's got into him.'

'Perhaps its the sunshine. Makes us all feel more cheerful.'

'Hm.' He pursed his lips, munching.

The weather was beautiful; day after day the sky was a deep clear blue with just enough cloud to give variety. In gardens and on Parliament Hill the grass began to look parched, and dustbins sometimes did not smell very nice. There was a plague of greenfly but the roses began to bloom magnificently nevertheless; and at night the cooling air released their scent and the scent of tobacco plant from the gardens Mr Didcot passed on his promenades. The hospital garden by the porter's lodge was especially fine; he made a point of always going past the hospital, partly to admire the flowers, mainly because that was where he was supposed to be, and had been for a time directly after the war, when he was younger, the strength of his arms and shoulders useful for portering, offsetting the flat feet that had kept him out of the Forces. His muscles had developed during his ARP services; he had dug and shovelled his way to many a battered body, his tin hat on the back of his head against the falling debris, his mouth tight shut against the dust, a terrier, quite without fear. Dead or alive, Mr Didcot got through to them. Stirring times.

The hospital had been something the same, the same sense of community, cups of tea, jolly girls, continual life and death, the same muscles, lugging or lifting, pushing or turning, trolleys of food or linen or people, to kitchen or operating theatre or mortuary. But not quite the same, for he wasn't a hero then; an unwieldy overall wasn't the same as a tin hat, gum boots, gas mask. He stayed till Nelly could draw her old age pension, went on part-time for a year or two more till he could draw his own; never went into the place again, though he always walked past it because that's where he was assumed to be, and a lot of what was wrong with this country today was a lack of integrity. So every evening when he left home he turned right towards the hospital, stepping briskly, rain or shine, past its gates and on to his own occupations.

In winter or in bad weather he took a sixpenny bus ride towards London, getting out in a district that did not know him although by now he knew it. There were cafés where young people gathered (no pubs, for he didn't approve of alcohol, which led to disgusting behaviour such as, when he was a schoolboy, his mother's had been) where, with a cup of tea and a doughnut, he could sit for a long time watching and listening to their filthy language, their squeals and guffaws, the jukebox's throbbing and disgusting words. Occasionally someone would notice him, jeer and bait him a little; then he would get up and leave; but mostly they were so absorbed in their own degenerate mating rituals, and he sat so small and quiet in his corner, that no one knew he was there.

If the weather was bad he would go to a cinema, sitting in the back row with his cap in his lap, his gaze on the screen, but his ears and senses alert to the groping, shifting, stertorous couples around him; sometimes the ushers flashed their torches along the seats, and that was a bonus. If the weather was good he would walk, not very fast, down streets where girls might loiter and sometimes speak, or down side roads and shady squares where railings and benches were sometimes rewarding. Not more than once a week he gave himself a special treat and spent the whole evening on the Hill and in the bushy Heath beyond. His eyes soon adjusted themselves to the dark and he did not need a torch. Silent, alert, he moved like a small grey animal from cover to cover.

Always, about eleven o'clock, he turned back. The pubs and cinemas had come out, there were too many people about and then not enough, everyone had to get home. The evening was over, and back past the hospital gates, into Wardlow Road, past the neglected privet, the whiffy dustbins, in through the rusted gate and the well oiled door, silently entering, hanging his cap, checking on Nelly's snores, going upstairs on delicate feet, testing the silence of Errol's sleep on the floor above, all's well, and the bedroom door shuts quietly on an evening enjoyably spent.

Except sometimes.

The newspapers headlined Drought. The kitchen window was open over the sink, the back door wide and the front door left ajar to catch a through draught, should one push its way through the sultry air. Sardines and a bit of lettuce were all they had felt like eating, and their cups of tea brought the sweat out like rain on their faces. Mr Didcot was in shirtsleeves, his Adam's apple unrestricted by collar and tie, and damp patches showed under Nelly's arms and down the back of her overall.

'Going up, are you?' she said, and he did not bother to answer for of course he was going up, he always did in the afternoons and it was too hot to engage in female trivia. He went upstairs and into the Den, shutting the door behind him. The sun was this side of the house, and he went to open the window, then drew the curtains half across to keep out the worst of it. The room was stuffy; it smelled of carpet and old newspapers and, very slightly, of gas, for the fire was old and its joints were not quite what they should be. With the curtains half-closed, the room was a cavern.

He went to his desk and switched on the light, sat down and shifted the piles of manuscript, drew a graph paper towards him, with pursed lips. Leaned back, drumming with his fingers, looking at the diagrams and the reproductions of royal portraits tacked to the wall; yawned, then belched modestly, switched off the lamp, got up and crossed to the divan; sat down, took off his shoes, lay back, unfastening the top button of his trousers with a small sigh of easement; his body settled into its imprint on the dusty covers, his head into the indented cushion, his heels into the hollow at the end. He lay staring up at the veined ceiling as the light waxed and waned with the sluggish movement of the curtain, relaxed in his cosy coffin. Thoughts came and went – pleasant ones, for he smiled a little, his eyelids closed, he drifted down the dark and soft familiar ways...

He woke suddenly. A breeze had come up and the curtains flapped to and fro. The angle of the sun was different; it must be mid-afternoon. He moved himself gingerly, stiff, working his mouth, which was dry and not very pleasant. A cup of tea would be nice. He put his feet to the floor, scratching himself here and there.

But what had awakened him?

A dream? Had he had a dream? But his afternoon dreams were always enjoyable ones, from which he surfaced slowly, the unreal and real blending, separating only with reluctance.

A noise? That must be it. Perhaps he had snored himself awake; but it had seemed sharper than that, exterior. He got to his feet and moved towards the window, pulling aside a curtain and looking out.

Nelly lay at the bottom of the shelter steps, a mound of flowered pinafore, half inside the open door of the Anderson.

He was out of the room, down the stairs, out into the garden before he knew it. She lay with her bottom and thick legs out in the sun, her head and shoulders in the darkness of the portal. The door of the shelter was only half open but a furious, steely glance showed him that enough could be seen – and there were other senses as well. He gave a great heave at her shoulders, got her outside the door and shut it swiftly, making no noise; the key was in the lock and he turned it, putting the key in his trouser pocket. He looked round and up, searching the windows of the neighbouring houses for faces staring but there were none, only the blank windows, the grimy bricks, the drainpipes and gutters and here and there a flowerpot with a plant straggled in it, a clothes-line slanting down like the rigging of an ill-found ship.

He looked down at the hulk at his feet, his face like a skull. Then he bent and began to tug her up the steps, her head lolling, her fat arms and legs dragging. She had cut her face when she fell and a small trickle of blood gleamed on her temple. She began to come to as he heaved and struggled, his lips thin as he panted, and began to make feeble efforts to help herself, her head going from side to side, gasps and muttered cries coming from her – 'Oh my God! Dad – wait a minute – oh God...' but he paid no attention, lugging her roughly over the grass, the back doorstep, inside the cover of the house. He let her go with a thump, straightening up and wiping his hand over his face. She lay on the linoleum, moaning and gasping, 'Oh God – oh Dad – oh my God . . .' Her stockings had been dragged down and she had lost a slipper.

After a moment, getting his breath, he said, 'Can you get up?'

She began to turn herself over onto her hands and knees and then to pull herself up against the wall and with her husband's hands. Supported by him, clinging to door and table, she managed to reach her chair in the kitchen, where he off-loaded her and stood back, taking a handkerchief from his trouser pocket and wiping his face and neck.

She lay inert, her eyes closed, the clay colour of her face marked by the line of blood, the lungs going like bellows under her big breasts.

'What made you do a silly thing like that, then?' he asked quietly.

She opened her eyes. 'The watering-can. I wanted the watering-can.'

'What for?'

'The ramblers – it's so dry. I thought I'd give them a water. Oh Arthur...'

'That's a silly blooming thing to do, isn't it? You know your legs won't carry you.'

'They've bin better. I've bin walking . . .'

'Where?'

'In the passage. Oh Arthur! There's something awful...'

'Did you go in?'

'I pushed open the door – and then...'

'Then you didn't see nothing, did you?'

'I did, I did! And the smell . . .' She began to cry, struggling to find a handkerchief among the cushions. 'Oh Arthur, there's something awful in there.'

After a moment he said, 'There's nothing in there.'

'There is, there is!'

'You didn't go inside. All old places smell funny when they've bin shut up a long time.'

'Not like that. It was awful . . .'

'Maybe a rat got in there, couldn't get out. Or a cat.'

'It wasn't a cat, Arthur. I could see . . .'

'See what?'

'Legs. Legs just laying there behind the door.' She began to sob and shriek a little, rocking about in the chair.

He caught her shoulder and pressed her back. 'Shut up! Do you want next door to hear you?'

'Oh! Oh!'

'This needs thinking about.' He sat down on a hard chair and stared out of the window, his lips pursed.

'What shall we do, Arthur?'

'Let me think.'

'We'll have to get the police.'

'I don't know as I want to do that.'

'But we must.'

'We need to keep clear heads about this. If you're right, that is. If you really saw . . .'

'I did, I did! I'll never forget it!'

'You saw just the one?'

'Oh my God, Arthur, is there more than one in

there?'

'There might be. I mean, we don't know, do we? If you're right about it at all, that is. What we have to ask ourselves is, how did they get there?'

She gaped at him, tears halted, the handkerchief clenched in her hands. He still stared out of the window, reflectively.

'I mean, there's no access from the back, is there? You wouldn't hardly have someone heaving a body over the wall into our garden, getting the key from our toilet and locking her up in our Anderson, would you? It seems to me it's got to be someone from inside this house.'

Now he looked at her, turning his trim head with a faint smile. 'It can't hardly be you, can it, even if you have kept quiet about your walking. And it can't hardly be me. So who does that leave us with?'

The colour surged up over her face and neck; she struggled more upright in the chair. 'Never!'

'Who else, then?'

'Never! Not my Errol. Never!'

'How d'you know? How can you tell? You don't know what goes on in that black head of his. We treat them like they was the same as us but they're savages really, most of them.'

'Not my Errol.'

'When you think of it, it's queer really, him never having any girl friends – handsome young chap like him. Not very bright upstairs, of course, but plenty downstairs I shouldn't wonder, from all I've heard about them. Suppose he's bin sneaking girls in here and went berserk? It could happen.'

'Never,' she whispered.

'We'd never know. Sleep like logs, the both of us, don't we? He could get up to all sorts of larks up there and we'd never know. He could get the key, shove her in there . . .'

'I never said it was a she.'

He looked at her sharply. 'You said legs.'

'We all got legs.'

'You said legs. If it'd bin a man you'd have said trousers.'

'It was trousers. But it was a girl's legs.'

'Well then . . .'

Staring at him, the flesh seemed to shrink on her cheeks. She opened her lips, no sound would come. It was very quiet.

'Get the police, Arthur.'

'I've told you, we need to keep a clear head.'

'We've got to.'

'We don't want to be hasty.'

She simply looked at him.

He got to his feet and moved about the room, touching the furniture, his lips, his thin hair. 'You get the police in, you've got a hornets' nest. You don't know where it'll end. You'll have police all over the place, digging, searching, turning everything upside down. A Roman circus, that's what you'll have, reporters ringing the doorbell, crowds outside staring, questions, newspaper photographs . . .'

She said nothing.

'We don't want that, do we? We don't want Errol

taken away and never see him again, do we, no matter what he's done. We don't know the rights of it, do we? If you and me keep our mouths shut, who's to know?'

'He will.'

'How? How'll he know?'

'If he done it, he knows already.'

'But he don't know *we* know.'

'Could you live like that? Looking at him and wondering?'

'I have command of my intellect. I don't let my heart rule my head like a silly woman.'

'He never done it, Arthur. Not my Errol. You know that.'

'Well, if he didn't, why tell him about it? Why not keep quiet?'

'And live with him in the house and that outside in the Anderson and never say nothing?'

'Why not?'

'I couldn't do it. I couldn't do it, Arthur.' She began to struggle forward in her chair. 'I couldn't live another day in this house, knowing what's out there in the shelter.'

He came behind her chair and put his hands on her shoulders, pressing her back against the cushions. 'Hold on, Mother, wait a minute. No need to get excited.' She lay panting under his hands, and he looked down at her, seeing her upside down, grizzled hair, pouched face, great breasts and arms and belly and legs in their trailing stockings, and her eyes looking up at him, upside down. 'What you going to do, then?'

'Tell Errol.'

'No.'

'We must, Arthur. It's only right.'

'No.'

He slid one hand from her shoulder across her neck under her chin, and with the other withdrew one of the cushions from behind her head and pressed it over her face. She slid down into the chair, threshing, but his arm held her inexorably, forcing her chin up into the dusty cushion which pressed, pressed, pressed over the mouth and eyes gaping hidden beneath it, as anaesthetists in the operating theatre pressed on the faces of their patient victims. Her fingers clawed at his arms but ineffectually, wild and emotional and silly as all women's gestures were, without plan or intelligence, merely a welter of flailing limbs, ugly limbs, swollen and long past their functions, as the sounds muffled by the cushion were functionless, so many animal grunts devoid of all but panic and hysteria. He watched this hulk heaving and shuddering under him, felt its useless spasms under his arms, felt a sweet and limpid power rise from the efforts of her body into his steely arms, his shoulders rigid and immovable, his face stern yet passionless, his mind soaring, soaring into a realm of radiant perception into which his body rose and followed, filling, rising, strengthening, bursting . . .

A blow blinded him, he was flung across the room and fell, clutching the sink. As he clung there two more blows caught him either side of the head, and he sank to his knees, bowed over, blinded and deaf, and a great pain shot into his ribs and another, and he bent himself over further still, curling up on the linoleum near the rubbish pail and the stack of old newspapers, the sink wall a cliff above him. The whirlwind left him, and opening his eyes he saw through the table legs Errol's plastic bag of laundry dropped on the floor by the door.

Errol was bent over Nelly, heaving her up, his long legs and her flopping arm a curious three-legged creature from where Mr Didcot lay. There was a puffing, gasping, muttered exhortations, the slither of feet, the chair creaking, whooping ugly sounds, a cry, sobs, and swear words dropping like small cold pebbles.

He began to pull himself slowly to his knees, his head thundering.

Errol swung round, hunched, hands clawed. 'What you done to her, you bastard?'

'Don't, Errol, don't!' Nelly wheezed, struggling up, clutching his jacket.

'I'll do you, you bastard, I'll do you!'

Mr Didcot's head had cleared, although he still felt its pain and the pain where Errol had kicked him. He managed to stand upright, hanging on to the edge of the sink. 'Like you done the others?'

'What others? Others . . .' The ferocity died out of Errol, leaving bewilderment and fear.

Nelly was crying and tugging at his side. 'In the shelter. There's something awful lying in the shelter . . .'

'What . . .?' He wet his lips. 'What you know about that?'

'She stuck her nose in where it wasn't wanted, son.' He straightened himself, despite the pain in his ribs, and smoothed his hair. 'Walking about, she's bin, and not telling anyone, and walked into something more than she bargained for.'

'I wanted the watering-can,' she whimpered.

'What she's seen out there I don't know, but I dare-say you do.'

'Me?'

'Yes, you, sonny boy.'

'Get the police, Errol.'

'That's what she keeps saying. Very well. You go and get them. And don't blame me when they put the handcuffs on you.'

'Me? It wasn't me!'

'Who was it then – me?' He stood quite jauntily now. 'Try telling them that and see where it gets you.'

'You . . .!' Errol lunged towards him but Mr Didcot dodged the other side of the table, the open door at his back. Nelly still clung to Errol's coat.

'I'll tell them, Errol, I'll tell them what he tried to do to me. Oh my God, I'll tell them, dear, I'll tell them . . .' She sank down in the chair, sobbing into her hands.

'You can try.' Mr Didcot smiled tolerantly. 'You can try and see what they make of it. But it's hardly likely they'll have much doubt between a respectable householder like I am and a nigger off the streets.'

Across the table they stared at one another.

'Ma,' Errol said at last, 'help me.'

'I'll help you, dear, I'll help you.'

'I never done it.'

'I know, dear, I know you didn't.'

'He's sharper than me. He's always bin after me.'

'I've bin after you, my lad, because I hoped to make something out of you – a silk purse out of a sow's ear, it seems.' Mr Didcot's voice was sharp. 'I hoped you might be able to benefit from my ideas, to absorb something of my great conceptions of life and history and the destinies of man; to raise yourself up out of the mud you come from and measure up a little to an intellect that's as far above yours as Everest is to a molehill. I hoped to show you wider horizons, better things, get you thinking big beyond what the usual run of ordinary people think. I hoped you'd be fit to be my disciple, to carry on my work after I'm gone, not in a creative sense, that'd be far beyond you, but to keep my thoughts alive. I hoped I could train you so's we'd be close, close, closer than what my boy could've bin because you're what you are, different, further to come, outlandish. I hoped that when I showed you my secrets you'd be worthy. I was mistaken.

He stood smiling contemptuously. His face was beginning to swell a little on one side and he touched it delicately. The sun was hazing over, and beyond the window the garden and the Anderson shelter were no longer golden but grey. The wind was coming up. It would rain later.

Errol said heavily, 'We'll go together. To the police.'

Mr Didcot stepped back. 'You think what you're doing, son.'

'I know what I'm doing.'

'They'll crucify you. They'll have a field day. You'll bring a hornets' nest about your head, it'll be the end of you.'

'You too. I don't care. You stay here, who knows what you'll do to Ma, to anyone – take them in off the streets like stray animals, throw them out again when you've done . . .'

'They'll believe me. They won't believe you. They'll be able to tell she was put there since you've bin here.'

'Not the first one wasn't.'

Nelly gave a cry, and Mr Didcot drew in his breath sharply, staring at Errol from a face tight and white as a bone.

'Right,' he said. He took his jacket from the chair-back where it had hung since lunch and put it on, buttoning it carefully. 'Right. I'll go alone. I don't need you. I'll tell my story first. I'll bring them back. Let them see for themselves. See the marks on me. She didn't do them, did she? I didn't do them myself, did I? Violence, see. And that cut on her face – who done that, eh? In fear of our lives, we've bin. Leaving her here with you, you'll have made her say anything. Who'll believe her, eh, when it's your word against mine?' He pulled his jacket straight, put back his shoulders. 'You black cunt,' he said, and went.

'Oh Errol, Errol!'

'Ma.' He turned slowly and dropped to his knees by the chair. They put their arms round each other and he rested his head against hers.

'I'll stand by you, dear, I'll stand by you.'

'He liked me.'

'I know he did, dear. But it's life or death now. He won't hesitate.'

After a while he said, 'He might not fetch them. He might cut and run.'

'He might. We'll have to see. We'll just have to wait and see.'

'I'm scared.'

She rocked him. 'Don't be scared. Don't be scared, Errol sweetheart. The innocent don't have nothing to fear.'